EX LIBRIS

VINTAGE **CLASSICS**

SIMONE DE BEAUVOIR

Simone de Beauvoir was born in Paris in 1908. In 1929 she became the youngest person ever to obtain the *agrégation* in philosophy at the Sorbonne, placing second to Jean-Paul Sartre. She taught at the lycées at Marseille and Rouen from 1931–1937, and in Paris from 1938–1943. After the war, she emerged as one of the leaders of the existentialist movement, working with Sartre on *Les Temps modernes*. The author of several books including *The Mandarins* (1957), which was awarded the Prix Goncourt, de Beauvoir was one of the most influential thinkers of her generation. She died in 1986.

LAUREN ELKIN

Lauren Elkin is the author of several books, including *Flâneuse: Women Walk the City*. Her co-translation (with Charlotte Mandell) of Claude Arnaud's biography of Jean Cocteau won the 2017 French-American Foundation's translation award. After twenty years in Paris, she now lives in London.

SIMONE DE BEAUVOIR

The Inseparables

TRANSLATED FROM THE FRENCH BY
Lauren Elkin

INTRODUCED BY
Deborah Levy

AFTERWORD BY
Sylvie Le Bon de Beauvoir

VINTAGE

3 5 7 9 10 8 6 4

Vintage is part of the Penguin Random House
group of companies whose addresses can be found at
global.penguinrandomhouse.com

Afterword © Éditions de L'Herne, 2020
English translation of novel, afterword and captions
© Lauren Elkin, 2021
Introduction © Deborah Levy, 2021

This edition first published in Great Britain by Vintage Classics, 2021
First published as *Les inséparables* by Simone de Beauvoir © 2020,
Éditions de l'Herne

Archive Material images: 1/3/5/6/9 © Association Élisabeth
Lacoin / Éditions de L'Herne; 2/7/8/10 © Collection Sylvie
Le Bon de Beauvoir; Image 4 Rights Reserved.

penguin.co.uk/vintage

A CIP catalogue record for this book is available from
the British Library

ISBN 9781784877002

Typeset in 12/14.75 pt Bembo
by Integra Software Services Pvt. Ltd, Pondicherry

Printed and bound in Great Britain by Clays Ltd, Elcograf S.p.A.

The authorised representative in the EEA is Penguin Random House
Ireland, Morrison Chambers, 32 Nassau Street, Dublin D02 YH68

Penguin Random House is committed to a sustainable future for
our business, our readers and our planet. This book is made from
Forest Stewardship Council® certified paper.

Introduction

This introduction contains plot spoilers.

In every decade of my life since my twenties, I have been awed, confused, intrigued and inspired by Beauvoir's attempt to live with meaning, pleasure and purpose. 'Be loved, be admired, be necessary; be somebody,' she insisted in her autobiography, *Memoirs of a Dutiful Daughter*.

The act of her writing what has now been titled *The Inseparables* cannot be extricated from this epic endeavour. It is a valuable part of the long conversation that Beauvoir's many books have begun with old and new readers.

After she'd won the Goncourt Prize for the immense reach of *The Mandarins*, I can see it must have been appealing for Beauvoir to write an intimate novella. *The Inseparables* once again returns to her friendship (from the age of nine) with Elisabeth Lacoin, nicknamed Zaza. Beauvoir's readers know that this friendship had long haunted her, not only in her books, but in her dreams.

In my view she never quite managed to write up the spectre of Zaza entirely convincingly, which is why she kept returning to try and catch her on the page. Maybe this is because her own fierce desire for Zaza to finally claim the life she deserved might have been stronger than Zaza's own desire to risk all she would lose in doing so: God, her family, bourgeois respectability.

Given that childhood is the beginning of everything we experience most deeply, it is not surprising that Beauvoir's strong feelings and hopes for Elisabeth Lacoin were also the beginning of her political education.

At the time they were at school together, women could not vote, were coerced into marriage and societally encouraged to accept an existence that mostly involved servicing the needs of their future husbands and children.

So, what sort of girl was Elisabeth Lacoin? Her avatar in *The Inseparables* is named Andrée, Beauvoir is Sylvie.

In her very first encounter at a private Catholic school with Sylvie, new pupil Andrée announces she was 'burned alive' while cooking potatoes at a campfire. Her dress caught alight and her right thigh was 'grilled to the bone'. Andrée's bold and playful tone is captured perfectly in Lauren Elkin's translation from the French. Elkin skilfully manages to convey, in pared-down prose, Andrée's beguiling sensibility and the ways in which Sylvie is enraptured by her forthright manner: her confidence, her cartwheels, her talent for literature, for playing the violin, riding a horse, mimicking teachers. Sylvie is bored and intellectually lonely, so meeting this clever, devout, but irreverent girl changes her life. Sylvie tells us, 'Nothing so interesting had ever happened to me. It suddenly seemed as if nothing had ever happened to me at all.'

Andrée tends to say tragic things in a way that deliberately does not invite sympathy. This is a clever narrative trick on Beauvoir's part. It means that Sylvie can do all the feeling for Andrée. She observes that her new friend does not speak to teachers in a humble manner, nor is she discourteous. In fact, she tells the female teacher that she is not intimidated by her. Why is that? It's not because she is above being intimidated, it's just that the teacher is not intimidating.

There is much that society will throw at Andrée to intimidate and flatten her, not least religion and the desire to not disappoint her controlling, conservative mother. And to make life as complicated as it actually is – which novelists must do – Andrée loves her mother. Sylvie can jealously see that all other attachments are not as important to her friend. How can she compete with this maternal bond, even usurp it?

When Sylvie, who hates needlework, goes to great effort to sew Andrée a silk bag for her thirteenth birthday present, she suddenly realises her friend's mother, Madame Gallard, doesn't like her anymore. Beauvoir hints that Andrée's mother understands that the sewing of the silk bag is a labour of love, and disapproves of these strong feelings for her daughter.

Sylvie falls in love with Andrée's mind. Obviously, her manner and liveliness make her body attractive too. Yet, this kind of cerebral love is subversive because for Beauvoir's generation (she was born in 1908) the minds of girls and women were not what made them valuable. The girls have long conversations together. They continue talking for twelve years. 'We could lose ourselves for hours in discussions of property, justice and equality. We had zero respect for our teachers' opinions, and our parents' ideas didn't satisfy us either.'

The talking cure between Andrée and Sylvie is nothing less than a revolution at a time when girls and women were encouraged to keep their thoughts to themselves. 'They teach you in catechism to respect your body. So selling your body in marriage must be as bad as selling it on the street,' Andrée says.

The enigma of female friendship that is as intense as a love affair, but that is not sexually expressed, or even particularly repressed, is always an interesting subject. Yet, while Sylvie, who is now a teenager, listens to Andrée speaking of her passion for her male cousin – she has taken up kissing him and now smokes Gauloises – she also owns her emotions.

'I suddenly understood, in a joyful stupor, that the empty feeling in my heart, the mournful quality of my days, had but one cause: Andrée's absence. Life without her would be death.'

Sylvie is endearingly vulnerable because she risks loving Andrée – and of course, any kind of love involves a fair dose of fantasy, projection, imagination. The idolised subject of her affection does not reciprocate the strength of her feelings, nor does she believe herself to be lovable. Meanwhile, Andrée's older sister, Malou, is being groomed for marriage with 'stupid and ugly' male suitors.

Madame Gallard's message to her daughters is clear: 'Join a convent or get a husband; remaining unmarried is not a vocation.'

What I find most touching in *The Inseparables* is the description of Sylvie losing her faith. In various interviews, Beauvoir described the experience of suddenly not believing in God as 'a kind of awareness'. Literature would eventually take the place of religion in her life and fill the void of an evaporated God.

When Sylvie is fourteen she realises during confession with the school priest that her relationship with God is changing. 'I don't believe in God! I said to myself . . . The truth of it stunned me for a moment: I didn't believe in God.'

The priest picks up on this new mood and chastises her.

'I have been told that my little Sylvie is not the same girl she was,' said the voice. 'It seems she has become distracted, disobedient and insolent.'

Instead of being apologetic, Sylvie becomes rebellious. With caustic wit, Beauvoir tells us that Sylvie was more shaken by her new lack of respect for this priest than by the man who had recently flashed her on the metro.

Andrée asks Sylvie an important question.

'If you don't believe in God, how can you bear to be alive?'

Sylvie replies, 'But I love being alive.'

Does Andrée love being alive? We know that she was nearly burned alive as a young girl. At her family's country house, to which Sylvie is invited, Andrée pushes herself so perilously high on a swing that Sylvie fears it will topple over. She wonders anxiously if 'something had broken inside her mind, and she couldn't stop'.

When she is again in dispute with her harassing mother and wishes to get out of a tedious family engagement, Andrée cuts a deep wound into her foot with an axe while chopping wood.

Suddenly someone cried out. The voice was Andrée's. I ran to the woodshed. Madame Gallard was leaning over her; Andrée was lying in the sawdust, bleeding from her foot; the edge of the axe was stained red.

When Andrée opens her eyes, she says, 'The axe got away from me!'

In the fairy tale, 'The Red Shoes', by Hans Christian Andersen, the female protagonist wears a beloved pair of red shoes to church. She is told that it is improper to do so, but she cannot resist. To cure her vanity, a magic spell is cast, in which, not only can she never take off her red shoes, but she is doomed to dance non-stop in them for ever. Eventually, she finds an executioner and asks him to chop off her feet. He obliges, but her amputated feet continue to dance on their own accord. 'Something had broken inside her mind and she couldn't stop.' Is Andrée her own executioner?

She needs to use the axe to separate from her mother, but instead turns it on herself. This scene is a prelude to what Beauvoir saw as the execution of Andrée Gallard by society.

By the time they study together for their exams at the Sorbonne, Andrée begins a romance with a fellow student, Pascal Blondel, the avatar for the phenomenologist, Maurice Merleau-Ponty. This relationship is disapproved of by her parents, who are keen to marry off their clever daughter. When Sylvie and Andrée meet for tea to discuss this forbidden (chaste) romance, Sylvie observes: 'All around me perfumed women ate cake and talked about the cost of living. From the day she was born, Andrée was fated to be like them. But she was nothing like them.'

Andrée does not become like them. She dies from meningitis instead, broken-hearted and defeated. Beauvoir saw her death as nothing less than murder. At the funeral, as Madame Gallard sobs, while her husband says, 'We have been but instruments in the hands of God', Sylvie places three red roses amongst the white roses heaped on her coffin, red as the blood that dripped from the axe. If she had always secretly thought that 'Andrée was one of those prodigies about whom, later on, books would be written', she was correct.

Simone de Beauvoir would write it, and here it is.

Deborah Levy, 2021

Translator's note

'So, is it any good?' people have asked me when I've told them I'm translating a 'lost' novel by Simone de Beauvoir, one she didn't publish in her lifetime, but didn't destroy before she died, either. And I am relieved to say: yes. It is more than good. It is poignant, chilling and eviscerating.

Beauvoir tells her story straightforwardly, without filler, building momentum as it reaches its inevitable conclusion, which will surprise no one familiar with Beauvoir's memoirs or diaries. 'For a long time, I believed that I had paid for my own freedom with her death,' she wrote of her childhood friend Elisabeth 'Zaza' Lacoin at the end of *Memoirs of a Dutiful Daughter* (1958). But in that book Zaza's story is one strand of a thickly braided account of Beauvoir's upbringing. *The Inseparables*, on the other hand, finished four years earlier, reads like the testimony of a witness to her murder.

I recognised more than a few passages from the memoirs. But here, they are given urgency by the taut, harrowing tale from which they emerge. In this sense it also feels like a statement Beauvoir has had to give several times to some authority – and in the absence of God there is no more punishing authority in this case than Beauvoir, condemning Zaza's family; her lover, the future famed phenomenologist Maurice Merleau-Ponty; and, not least, herself. Readers of a more psychoanalytic bent may find the repetitions in the stories to be telling. But nowhere else does Beauvoir tell her story with Zaza so fully, imagining with such love (though utterly without nostalgia) the life they shared and the vanished world that contained her friend.

Nevertheless, it would be doing Beauvoir as novelist a disservice to read *The Inseparables* only as a work of memoir or therapy. This is a deliberately patterned, attentively sculpted narrative, streamlined and disciplined where the memoirs are digressive, and unified in its plot, its treatment of the girls' friendship and its religious, punitive vocabulary. An accident that might elsewhere be described (sarcastically) as 'fortuitous' is instead 'providential'; the word 'reproach' or its corollary 'irreproachable' figures some eleven times in the original French, and on eight of those occasions I chose to keep rather than vary it. *Devoir*, which can mean 'homework' or 'obligation', appears many times in the text; English unfortunately does not allow us to preserve the way the meaning of that word shifts for Andrée from childhood to young adulthood. Likewise, the tone of the novel evolves with the girls as they mature, and I have tried to do justice to this as well.

There is a lot of dialogue in the book; what Sylvie and Andrée love to do more than anything else is discuss things with each other – love, family, philosophy, God – and I have mostly reproduced these discussions as they are in the French. However, where they began to feel stilted, or gratuitous, or simply as unequivocal as an assent, I've shaded them into indirect speech. We are so much in Sylvie's mind, in her account of what transpired, that I don't think it poses a problem to make some of the dialogue internal.

I have tried to keep an element of formality in these conversations, because however close friends they may be, they call each other the formal *vous*. When they see each other after a long separation, they shake hands instead of kissing on the cheek. But, as they tell one of Andrée's little sisters: you can have a very close friend and not embrace them.

And this for me is the crux of the novel. *The Inseparables* has much to teach us about women's history, and the conflict of feminism and religion, but above all it is a novel about friendship between girls, or young women. Witnessing the way her best friend was crushed by the social system planted the seed for Beauvoir's major feminist work to come.

I wonder what happened to Zaza's little sisters. They must certainly have gone on to hear about Simone de Beauvoir;

I doubt there was a woman in France who hadn't heard of her. Did they put the famous philosopher together with the bookish, slightly frumpy young woman who was their sister's friend? Did they sneak a peek at *The Second Sex* in some bookshop? Perhaps if they're still alive they might pick up a copy of *The Inseparables* and find out what an impact Zaza had on one of the most important feminist statements of the twentieth century.

Lauren Elkin, 2021

The Inseparables

For Zaza

If there are tears in my eyes tonight, is it because you are no longer alive, or because I am? I should dedicate this story to you, but I know that you no longer exist anywhere, and my writing to you like this is pure literary artifice. In any case, this isn't really your story, only one inspired by us. You were not Andrée; nor was I Sylvie, who speaks in my name.

PART ONE

When I was nine years old I was a good little girl, though this hadn't always been the case. As a small child the adults' tyranny caused me to throw such tantrums that one of my aunts declared, quite seriously: 'Sylvie is possessed by a demon.' War and religion tamed me. Right away I demonstrated perfect patriotism by stomping all over my doll because she was made in Germany, though I didn't really care for her to begin with. I was taught that God would only protect France if I were obedient and pious: there was no escaping it. The other girls and I would walk through the basilica of Sacré-Cœur, waving banners and singing. I began to pray frequently, and I developed a real taste for it. Abbé Dominique, the chaplain at the Collège Adelaïde where we went to school, encouraged my ardour. Dressed all in tulle, with a bonnet made of Irish lace, I made my First Communion, and from that day forward, I set a perfect example for my little sisters. Heaven heard my prayers, and my father was appointed to a desk job at the Ministry of War because of his heart trouble.

That morning I was especially excited because it was the first day of school. I couldn't wait to get back to the classroom, solemn as a Mass; the silence in the hallways; the softened smiles of the teachers, in their long skirts and their high-necked blouses, who were often dressed as nurses since the school had been partially turned into a hospital. Under their white veils with red stains, they resembled saints, and I was overcome when they pressed me to their bosoms. I wolfed down the soup and grey bread which had replaced the hot chocolate and brioches from the pre-war days, and impatiently waited for my mother to finish dressing my sisters. All three of us wore sky-blue coats, made of real officer's serge and cut exactly like military greatcoats. 'Look! there's even a little martingale at the back,' my mother would show her friends, who were admiring, or taken aback. My mother held my sisters' hands as we left the building. We walked with sadness past Café La Rotonde, which had just opened noisily beneath our window, and which was, Papa said, a hang-out for defeatists. I found the word intriguing. 'Defeatists are people who believe that France will lose the war,' Papa explained. 'They should all be shot.' I didn't understand. We don't believe what we believe on purpose; can you really be punished for the things you think? The spies who handed out poisoned sweets to children, or pricked Frenchwomen with needles full of venom in the metro – obviously they deserved to die, but the defeatists baffled me. I didn't bother asking Maman; she always said the same thing as Papa.

My little sisters walked slowly; the wrought-iron grill of the Luxembourg Gardens seemed to go on for ever. Finally I arrived at the school gate and climbed the front stairs, joyfully trundling my satchel overflowing with new books. I recognised the faint odour of illness, mingled with the smell of wax on the freshly polished floors. The teachers kissed me. In the cloakroom I was reunited with my schoolmates from last year; I didn't have any particular attachments among them, but I liked the noise we all made together. I dawdled in the main hall, looking at the display cases full of old dead things that came here to die a second time – the feathers fell from the stuffed birds, the dried plants turned to dust, the shells lost their shine. When the bell rang, I entered the classroom they called Sainte-Marguerite. All the rooms looked the same; the students sat around an oval table covered in black moleskin, which would be presided over by our teacher; our mothers sat behind us and kept watch while knitting balaclavas. I went over to my stool and saw the one next to it was occupied by a hollow-cheeked little girl with brown hair, whom I didn't recognise. She looked very young; her serious, shining eyes focused on me with intensity.

'So you're the best student in the class?'

'I'm Sylvie Lepage,' I said. 'What's your name?'

'Andrée Gallard. I'm nine. If I look younger it's because I got burned alive and didn't grow much after that. I had to stop studying for a year but Maman wants me to catch up on what I missed. Can you lend me your notebooks from last year?'

'Yes,' I said.

Andrée's confidence and rapid, precise speech unnerved me. She looked me over warily. 'That girl said you're the best student in the class,' she said, tilting her head a little at Lisette. 'Is that true?'

'I often come in first,' I said, modest. I stared at Andrée, with her dark hair falling straight down around her face, and an ink spot on her chin. It's not every day that you meet a little girl who's been burned alive. There were so many questions I wanted to ask her, but Mademoiselle Dubois came in, her long dress sweeping the floorboards. She was a lively, moustachioed woman whom I greatly respected. She sat down and called the register. When she reached Andrée's name, she asked: 'Well, my girl, I hope we're not intimidating you?'

'I am not timid, Mademoiselle,' said Andrée with composure, adding, in a friendly voice, 'anyway, you are not intimidating.'

Mademoiselle Dubois hesitated for a moment, then smiled under her moustache and carried on.

When the day was over, leaving the classroom followed an unvarying ritual: Mademoiselle stood in the doorway and shook every mother's hand and kissed each pupil's forehead. She put a hand on Andrée's shoulder.

'You've never been to school before?'

'No, until today I studied at home, but now I'm too big for that.'

'I hope you will follow in your sister's footsteps,' Mademoiselle said.

'Oh!' said Andrée. 'We are very different. Malou takes after Papa, she loves maths, but I love literature the most.'

Lisette squeezed my elbow. It wasn't that Andrée was impertinent, exactly, but she wasn't addressing Mademoiselle in the tone you use to speak to a teacher.

'Do you know where to find the classroom for day girls? If no one comes to collect you on time, you can sit there while you wait,' said Mademoiselle.

'No one is coming to collect me; I go home by myself,' said Andrée, adding brightly: 'Maman said it's alright.'

'All by yourself?' asked Mademoiselle Dubois. 'Well, if your mother says so ...'

She kissed my forehead in turn, and I followed Andrée to the cloakroom. She slipped on her coat. It was less original than mine, but very pretty nonetheless, made of red ratine with gold buttons. She was no street urchin – how was she permitted to go out all alone? Was her mother unaware of the dangers? Had she not heard about the poisoned sweets and needles?

'Where do you live, dear?' Maman asked Andrée as we went down the stairs with my little sisters.

'Rue de Grenelle.'

'In that case,' said Maman, 'we can accompany you to the Boulevard Saint-Germain. It's on our way.'

'I would greatly appreciate it,' said Andrée, 'but please don't trouble yourself on my account.' She gave Maman a solemn look. 'You see, Madame, there are seven of us brothers and sisters; my mother says that we must learn to look after ourselves.'

Maman nodded, but her disapproval was visible.

As soon as we were in the street, I interrogated Andrée. 'How did you get burned?'

'While cooking potatoes on a campfire. My dress caught fire and my right thigh was grilled to the bone.' Andrée made a little impatient gesture; this old story bored her. 'When can I see your notebooks? I need to know what you studied last year. Tell me where you live and I'll come over this afternoon, or tomorrow.'

I looked enquiringly at Maman; when I went to the Luxembourg Gardens she didn't allow me to play with little girls I didn't know.

'This week won't be possible,' Maman said, with a hint of embarrassment in her voice. 'We can discuss it further on Saturday.'

'Very well, I'll wait till Saturday,' said Andrée.

I watched her cross the boulevard in her red ratine coat; she really was very small, but she walked with the confidence of a grown-up.

'Your Uncle Jacques knew some Gallards who were related by marriage to the Lavergnes, the Blanchards' cousins,' said Maman in a thoughtful voice. 'I wonder if it's the same family. But it seems to me that the right sort of people wouldn't let a nine-year-old girl roam the streets on her own.'

My parents discussed at great length the various branches of the various Gallard families of whom they had direct or indirect knowledge. Maman found out more from the teachers at school. Andrée's parents were only loosely connected with Uncle Jacques's Gallards, but they were perfectly good people. Monsieur Gallard had attended the École Polytechnique[1], had a good job at Citroën and was the president of the League of Fathers of Large Families; his wife, who was born a Rivière de Bonneuil, came from a great dynasty of militant Catholics, and was greatly respected by the parishioners of Saint-Thomas d'Aquin. No doubt apprised of my mother's hesitations, Madame Gallard picked

---

[1] One of the prestigious grandes écoles, entered through a competitive exam. Polytechnique, or X as it's nicknamed, was founded in 1794 and is a military school training France's most elite engineers, many of whom go on to lead the country.

Andrée up from school the following Saturday. She was a beautiful dark-eyed woman, whose black velvet collar was fastened with an antique brooch. She won over Maman by telling her she could pass for my older sister, and calling her *petite madame*. As for me, I never liked her velvet collar.

Madame Gallard obligingly recounted to Maman the story of Andrée's martyrdom: the fissured flesh, the enormous blisters, the sterilised bandages, Andrée's delirium and courage; while playing nearby, one of her little friends had accidentally kicked her, which reopened her wounds; she had made such an effort not to cry out that she fainted. When she came over to see my schoolbooks, I looked at her with respect; she took notes in her pretty, already well-formed handwriting, and I thought of her swollen thigh under her little pleated skirt. Nothing so interesting had ever happened to me. It suddenly seemed as if nothing had ever happened to me at all.

All the children I knew bored me, but Andrée made me laugh when we walked in the playground between classes. She was a perfect little mimic – she could do Mademoiselle Dubois's brusque movements, or the unctuous voice of Mademoiselle Vendroux, the headmistress. And she knew all sorts of little secrets about the place from her older sister: the teachers were affiliated with the Jesuits; they wore their hair parted on the side while they were novices, and in the middle once they'd taken their vows. Mademoiselle Dubois, at just thirty years old, was the

youngest; she had only obtained her baccalaureate the previous year, the older students had seen her at the Sorbonne,
blushing and embarrassed by her skirts. I was a bit shocked
by Andrée's irreverence, but I found her funny, and played
along when she improvised a dialogue between two of our
teachers. Her imitations were so accurate that often in the
middle of class we would elbow one another as we watched
Mademoiselle Dubois open the register or close a book;
once I was overcome with uncontrollable laughter to such
a point that I would surely have been shown the door had
my conduct not been, up to that point, so perfectly beyond
reproach.

The first few times I went to Andrée's home in the
rue de Grenelle to play, I was alarmed; in addition to her
many brothers and sisters, there was always a bevy of
cousins and visiting friends. They ran, shouted, sang and
disguised themselves; they jumped on tables, and overturned
furniture. Sometimes Malou, aged fifteen and full of her
own importance, complained, but we soon heard Madame
Gallard's voice, telling her to let us children amuse ourselves. I was amazed by her indifference to wounds, bumps,
stains, broken plates. 'Maman never gets angry,' Andrée told
me with a triumphant smile. At the end of the afternoon,
Madame Gallard, smiling, entered the wreckage of the
room, set a chair to right and blotted Andrée's forehead.
'Look at you, dripping with sweat again!' Andrée pressed
against her and for a moment her face was transformed.

I turned my eyes away with a sick feeling that was doubtless informed by jealousy, or perhaps envy, and the kind of fear inspired by things you don't understand.

I had been brought up to love Maman and Papa equally; Andrée made no secret of the fact that she preferred her mother to her father. 'Papa is too serious,' she told me one day. Monsieur Gallard made me uneasy because he was nothing like my own father. Papa never went to Mass, and if someone mentioned the miracles of Lourdes in his presence he would only smile. I had heard him say there was only one religion: the love of France. His impiety didn't bother me, and my mother, who was very pious, seemed to find it normal. A man as superior as Papa necessarily had more complicated dealings with God than women and little girls did. Monsieur Gallard, on the other hand, took Communion every Sunday with his family, wore a long beard and pince-nez, and during his free time performed charitable works. His silky hair and Christian virtue feminised him, and lowered him in my estimation. At any rate, we didn't see him very often; it was Madame Gallard who ruled over the house. I envied the freedom she gave Andrée, but however kindly she spoke to me, I was always uncomfortable around her.

Sometimes Andrée would say she was tired of playing, and we would go and sit in Monsieur Gallard's office. We sat in the dark, so we wouldn't be discovered, and talked.

It was a new pleasure. My parents talked, and I talked to them, but we didn't talk together; with Andrée, I had real conversations, like Papa in the evenings with Maman. She had read many books while she was convalescing. But what was incredible was that she seemed to think the stories they told had really happened. She hated Horace and Polyeucte and admired Don Quixote and Cyrano de Bergerac as if they had existed in flesh and blood.[2] When it came to centuries past, she also had pronounced preferences. She loved the Greeks but the Romans bored her; she cared little for the misfortunes of Louis XVII and his family, but the death of Napoleon deeply moved her.

Many of her opinions were subversive, but because she was so young, the teachers forgave her. 'This child has a lot of personality,' they said at school. Andrée quickly caught up on what she had missed; I just barely beat her at composition and she was given the honour of copying two of her essays into the *livre d'or*. She played piano so well that she was placed in the intermediate group, and soon began to study the violin as well. She didn't like to sew, but she was skilled at it; she was a very competent maker of caramels, *sablé* biscuits and chocolate truffles; although she was delicate, she could do the splits and turn

[2] Horace and Polyeucte are the eponymous characters in plays by Corneille.

a cartwheel and all sorts of somersaults. But what I admired most about her were the little habits she had that I never understood. Like when she saw a peach or an orchid, or even if someone just said one of those words to her, she shivered, and gooseflesh stood out on her arms. It was in those moments that I was most troublingly aware of the gift she had received from heaven, which I found so enthralling: her personality. Secretly I thought to myself that Andrée was one of those prodigies about whom, later on, books would be written.

★★★

The bombs and Big Bertha drove most of the students at school to leave Paris towards the middle of June. The Gallards went to Lourdes; every year they took part in a large pilgrimage. Their eldest son was a stretcher-bearer, while the daughters washed dishes with their mother in a hospice kitchen. It impressed me that Andrée was given such adult tasks, and I respected her all the more. However, I was proud of my parents' heroic stubborn refusal to leave Paris; by staying there we were showing our valiant soldiers that the civilians were holding down the fort. Along with an idiotic twelve-year-old, I was the only student left in our class, and I felt important. One morning, when I arrived at school, the teachers and students had taken refuge in the cellar. We laughed long and hard about that when I got home. When the sirens went off, we stayed where we were; the tenants from upstairs took shelter at ours, sleeping on sofas in the front parlour. All this hullabaloo was very exciting.

I left for Sadernac in late July with my mother and sisters. Grand-père, who remembered the siege of '71, was convinced we were eating rats in Paris, and for two months he stuffed us full of chicken and clafoutis.[3] Those were happy days. In the salon there was a bookcase full of old books whose pages were spotted with age; the forbidden ones were stashed way up top, but I was allowed to rummage freely through the lower shelves. I read, I played with my sisters, I went for walks. I walked a lot that summer. I wandered through chestnut groves and cut my fingers on the sharp ferns; all along the sunken paths I collected bouquets of honeysuckle and spindle; I tasted blackberries, strawberries, dogwood berries and acidic barberries; I inhaled the rough perfume of the flowering buckwheat and laid down on the ground to surround myself with the intimate scent of the heather. Then I would go and sit in the open fields, at the foot of the silver-leafed poplars, and open a novel by James Fenimore Cooper. When the wind blew, the poplars murmured. I was ecstatic. It seemed that from one end of the earth to

[3] Paris was under siege from the Prussian army from 19 September 1870 to 28 January 1871.

the other the trees were talking to God and to one another. The sound was musical, and prayer-like, and it journeyed through my heart before continuing on its way to heaven.

My pleasures were infinite, but difficult to describe; I sent only brief postcards to Andrée. She didn't write very much either; she was in the Landes, with her maternal grandmother; she rode horses; she was having a lot of fun; she wouldn't be back in Paris before mid-October. I didn't think of her often. During the summer holidays, I hardly thought at all of my life back in Paris.

I shed a few tears as I bid adieu to the poplars; I was getting older, and more sentimental. But in the train, I remembered how much I loved the autumn and going back to school. Papa was waiting for us at the train station in his sky-blue uniform. He said the war was nearly over. My schoolbooks seemed even newer than they had in other years: they were bigger and more beautiful; they cracked beneath my fingers and they smelled good. In the Luxembourg Gardens there was a stirring scent of dead leaves and burning grass; the teachers embraced me warmly and reserved their highest praises for the homework I'd done over the summer. So why was I so miserable? In the evenings, after dinner, I sat in the front parlour, reading, or writing stories in my notebook. My sisters were asleep; at the end of the hallway Papa was reading aloud to Maman. It was one of the best moments of the day. And then I would sprawl out on the red carpet, in a daze, doing absolutely nothing. I stared at the old Norman armoire and the sculpted wooden clock which held within its belly two copper pine cones and all the darkness of time. Against the wall stood the iron heater, its mouth gaping open, the tepid warmth of its nauseating breath emanating from its depths. In the dark, surrounded by all these mute objects, I was suddenly afraid. I heard Papa's voice; I knew he was reading from Gobineau's *Essay on the Inequality of Human Races*. The previous year it had been *The Origins of Contemporary France* by Hippolyte Taine.[4] The following year he would begin a new book, and I would still be here, between the armoire and the clock. How many years? How many evenings? Was this life, then? Killing time, one day after the next? Would I

[4] Joseph Arthur de Gobineau (1816–1882) – whom Beauvoir refers to as 'le comte de Gobineau' (the count of Gobineau) – was responsible for theorising a master Aryan race superior to all other peoples; his writings influenced Nazi and fascist ideology in Europe as well as white supremacy in the US. Hippolyte Taine (1828–1893) was a positivist philosopher; *The Origins of Contemporary France* is a six-volume history which looks at the evolution of the French state and its institutions from the ancien régime to the present day (he began it during the Franco-Prussian war of 1870; it was published from 1875–1893) and the steady current of violence that runs beneath the surface of everyday life, threatening to convulse into revolution at any moment.

go on in this state of boredom until I died? I told myself I was missing Sadernac; before I went to sleep, I shed a few tears for the poplars.

Two days later, I realised the truth in a flash of understanding. I entered the salle Sainte-Catherine and Andrée smiled at me. I smiled back and held out my hand. 'When did you get back?'

'Last night.' Andrée looked at me with a hint of malice. 'I assume you were here the very day classes resumed?'

'Yes,' I said. 'Did you have a good summer holiday?' I added.

'Very good, and you?'

'Very good.'

We spoke in banalities, like grown-ups, but I suddenly understood, in a joyful stupor, that the empty feeling in my heart, the mournful quality of my days, had but one cause: Andrée's absence. Life without her would be death. Mademoiselle de Villeneuve sat in her chair, and I repeated to myself: 'Without Andrée, I would no longer be alive.' My joy turned to anguish. What would become of me, I thought, if she died? I would be sitting here on this stool, the headmistress would enter and she would say in a serious voice: 'Let us pray, children; your little classmate Andrée Gallard was called home to God last night.' Well! it's very simple, I decided; I would slip from my stool and die as well. The thought of it didn't frighten me, as we would soon be reunited at the gates of heaven.

On the 11th of November we celebrated the armistice. People were kissing in the streets. For four years I'd prayed for that day to come, and expected enormous transformations when it did; I was flooded with hazy memories of the time before. Papa changed back into civilian clothes, but nothing much else happened. He talked endlessly about a certain capital city that had been plundered by Bolsheviks; these faraway men whose name sounded dangerously close to the *Boches*[5] seemed to possess terrifying powers. Meanwhile Foch had really let himself be manipulated; he should have driven his troops into Berlin itself. Papa took such a dark view of the future that he didn't dare to reopen his office; instead he found a position in an insurance company and informed us that we were going to have to tighten our belts. Maman gave notice to Élisa (who in any case was behaving very badly, going out with firemen in the evenings) and took over the housework herself. In the evenings she was sullen and bad-tempered, as was Papa; my sisters cried a lot. But it was all the same to me, as long as I had Andrée.

Andrée was getting taller and stronger, and I stopped thinking she might die. But another danger loomed: the school did not look kindly on our friendship. Andrée was a brilliant student; if I still came in first place it was because she was too haughty to compete for it. I envied her

[5] French slang for Germans.

indifference without being able to reproduce it. But she had fallen out of favour with the teachers. They found her contradictory, sarcastic, prideful, bad-spirited; they were never able to catch her being outright insolent because she remained carefully aloof, and that is perhaps what irritated them the most.

They scored a point the day of the piano recital. The auditorium was full. In the first few rows sat all the students, in their prettiest dresses, hair curled and tied up with bows; behind them were the teachers and tutors in silk blouses and white gloves; and then beyond them the parents sat with their guests. Andrée, dressed up in a blue taffeta frock, performed a piece that her mother thought was too difficult for her, and which in places she usually massacred. I felt for her, with all these more or less adversarial gazes fixed on her, as she approached a difficult section. She pulled it off without a single mistake, and, looking triumphantly over at her mother, stuck out her tongue. The little girls trembled beneath their hair ribbons, and the mothers coughed in outrage; the teachers exchanged glances and the headmistress was bright red. When Andrée came down from the stage, she ran to her mother and kissed her, laughing so joyously that Mademoiselle Vendroux didn't dare admonish her. But a few days later, she complained to my mother about Andrée's bad influence on me: we chattered in class, I giggled and was distracted. She talked about sitting us apart from each other, and I spent a week in agony. But my studiousness pleased Madame Gallard, and she convinced Maman to leave us in peace. Because our families were excellent clients of the school – Maman with her three daughters and Madame Gallard with six, and copious charm and diplomacy – we were permitted to continue sitting next to each other as we always had done.

Would Andrée have been sad if we had been prevented from seeing each other? Less than I would have been, to be sure. They called us the inseparables, and she preferred my company to that of the other girls. But it seemed to me that her love for her mother made her other attachments pale by comparison. Her family was enormously important to her. She spent hours amusing her twin baby sisters, bathing and dressing their chubby undifferentiated flesh, deciphering their babbling and hesitant mimicry, cuddling them and lavishing them with love. Then, too, there was her music. When she sat at the piano, or nestled her violin in the crook of her neck, listening reverently to the song that took shape beneath her fingers, I thought I heard her talking to herself; next to the unending dialogue that took place in the secrecy of her heart, our conversations seemed truly childish. Sometimes she would be accompanied on the piano by Madame Gallard, who played very well herself, and I would feel completely left out. No, our friendship was not as important to Andrée as it was to me, but I admired her too much to suffer from it.

The following year, we moved out of the apartment on the Boulevard Montparnasse and into a cramped flat in the rue Cassette where I no longer had so much as a corner to myself. Andrée invited me to come and work at her house as often as I liked. Every time I entered her room, I had an overwhelming impulse to make the sign of the cross. A crucifix hung above her bed, along with a sprig of box tree leaves, while Da Vinci's Saint Anne hung on the opposite wall; on the mantelpiece stood a portrait of Madame Gallard and a photograph of the château de Béthary. Her personal library lined the shelves: *Don Quixote*, *Gulliver's Travels*, *Eugénie Grandet*, and *Tristan and Isolde* from which she'd memorised entire passages. She usually preferred books of realism or satire, so her weakness for the romantic epic perplexed me.

I anxiously studied the walls and the objects that surrounded her. I would have liked to understand the things she said as her bow went dancing along the strings of her violin. I would have liked to know why, when she had so much love in her life, and so much talent, and things to keep her occupied, she so often wore a faraway, even melancholy air. She was very pious. When I sometimes went to pray in the chapel, often I would find she had arrived there first, on her knees before the altar, her head in her hands, or reaching out her arms towards a station of the cross. Was she contemplating one day taking her vows? And yet she so loved her freedom, and the joys of this world. Her eyes shone when she told me about her holidays, how she spent hours galloping on horseback through the forests of pine trees, getting scratched by their branches as she went, how she swam through still waters in ponds, or in the freshwater of the Adour river. Was she dreaming about that paradise when she sat motionless before her notebooks, with a lost look in her eye? One day she saw me observing her and she laughed, abashed. 'Do you think I'm wasting my time?'

'Me? Not at all!'

She gave me a somewhat superior look. 'Do you never find yourself daydreaming about something or other?'

'No,' I said, humbled. What would I have daydreamed about? I loved Andrée above all else, and she was right next to me.

I didn't daydream. I kept up rigorously with my school-work and Andrée made fun of me, a little; she more or less made fun of everyone, and I met her ridicule with good humour. Once, however, she cut me to the quick. That year, unusually, I had spent the Easter holidays in Sadernac. It was the first time I'd really seen what spring could be, and it dazzled me. I sat at a table in the garden with a stack of paper and for two hours I wrote a letter to Andrée in which I described the newly sprouted grass speckled with cowslip and primrose, the scent of the wisteria, the blue of the sky and all the transports of my soul. She didn't reply. When I saw her again in the school cloakroom, I asked her, reproachfully, 'Why didn't you write to me? Didn't you get my letter?'

'I got it,' she said.

'Well aren't you a lazy old thing!' I said.

Andrée started to laugh. 'I thought perhaps you'd accidentally sent me your homework instead of a letter.'

I felt myself redden. 'My homework?'

'Come on, you didn't squeeze out that literary masterpiece for me alone!' said Andrée. 'I was sure it was the first draft of an essay assignment: "Describe spring."'

'No,' I said. 'It was not quite a masterpiece, but I wrote it for you alone.' The little Boulard girls came over to us, curious and talkative, and we left it at that. But once we were in class I muddled up my Latin commentary. Andrée had found my letter ridiculous, and this was painful; but above all, she didn't see the extent to which I needed to share everything with her. That was what upset me the most: the realisation that she was utterly unaware of my feelings for her.

We left school together; Maman didn't come with me to school anymore, and usually I went home with Andrée. Suddenly she took hold of me by the elbow, something she'd never done before: usually we kept ourselves at a more formal distance.

'Sylvie, I'm sorry for what I said before,' she said urgently. 'It was pure spitefulness. I knew very well that your letter wasn't a piece of homework.'

'I suppose it was ridiculous,' I said.

'Not at all! The truth is, I was in a terrible mood when I received it, whereas you sounded so – exuberant!'

'Why were you in a bad mood?' I asked.

She was silent for a moment. 'I just was, it was nothing, or rather it was everything.' She hesitated. 'I'm fed up with being a child,' she said abruptly. 'Doesn't it seem like it will never end, to you?'

I looked at her, astonished. Andrée had so much more freedom than I had, and though things weren't exactly joyful at home, I was in no hurry to get older. The idea that I was already thirteen terrified me.

'No,' I said. 'Grown-ups' lives seem so monotonous – their days are all the same, no one ever learns anything new ...'

'There's more to life than learning!' Andrée said, impatient. I wanted to say yes, there's more to life than learning: there's you. But the conversation had shifted. I thought to myself, distressed, that in books there are people who make declarations of love, or hate, who dare to say whatever comes into their mind, or heart – why is it so impossible to do the same thing in real life? I would go without food or drink for two days and two nights to spend a mere hour with Andrée, or to spare her some hurt, and she doesn't realise it at all!

For several days I brooded over these thoughts, until I had an epiphany: I would make Andrée something for her birthday.

Parents are unpredictable beings; ordinarily, Maman found my little projects absurd before I could even explain them, but in this case she said yes straight away. I decided to make Andrée a hand-bag, following a pattern in *La Mode Pratique*, which I was determined would be the height of luxury. I chose red and blue silk with a shimmering, thick gold brocade (which in my eyes was as beautiful as a fairy tale) and assembled it on a woven wicker frame I made myself. I hated to sew, but I worked so assiduously that when the little purse was finished, it looked truly beautiful, with its cherry-coloured satin lining and its pleats. I wrapped it in tissue paper, laid it in a box and tied it with a ribbon.

The day Andrée turned thirteen, Maman and I went to her birthday party; it was already crowded when we arrived, and I felt intimidated as I handed the box to Andrée. 'It's for your birthday,' I said. She looked at me with surprise, and I added: 'I made it.'

She unwrapped the little red bag and, as she did, some colour rose in her cheeks. 'Sylvie! It's marvellous! How kind of you!' It seemed as though if our mothers hadn't been there, she would have kissed me.

'Thank Madame Lapage as well,' said Madame Gallard, in her society-lady's voice. 'Because it was certainly she who went to all the trouble.'

'Thank you Madame,' Andrée said curtly. And she smiled at me again, clearly moved. While Maman protested weakly, I felt a pit form in my stomach. I had just realised that Madame Gallard didn't like me anymore.

***

Today I admire the woman's vigilance and perceptiveness. The truth is, I was changing. I began to find our teachers profoundly stupid, and I kept myself amused by asking them embarrassing questions. I stood up to them, and made impertinent replies. Maman scolded me a bit, but when I told Papa about it, he only laughed. His laughter alleviated any qualms I might have had, though at the same time I didn't think for a second that God could be offended by my misconduct. When I went to confession, as I did several times a week, I didn't embarrass myself by recounting the sins of a child. Abbé Dominique encouraged me on the path to mystical contemplation, and my everyday life had nothing to do with this sacred adventure. The errors I admitted were those of the soul above all: I had lacked fervour, too long forsaken the divine presence, prayed inattentively, regarded myself too complacently.

I had just finished enumerating these failings when I heard the voice of Abbé Dominique ask, through the screen, 'Are you sure that's all?'

I couldn't speak.

'I have been told that my little Sylvie is not the same girl she was,' said the voice. 'It seems she has become distracted, disobedient and insolent.'

My cheeks burned; I couldn't bring myself to say a word.

'Starting today, we must guard against these things,' said the voice. 'We will discuss them together.' Abbé Dominique absolved me, and as I walked out of the confessional my head was spinning; I fled the chapel without doing my penitence. I was more shaken than that day on the metro when a man had spread open his overcoat to reveal something pink.

For eight years I had knelt before Abbé Dominique as before God, and here he had shown himself to be nothing but a gossipy old man, chit-chatting with the teachers and taking their blather seriously. I was ashamed to have bared my soul to him: he had betrayed me. From that day on, whenever I spotted his black robes in the corridor, I blushed and ran away.

The rest of the year, and the one after, I confessed to the priests at Saint-Sulpice, alternating between them. I continued to pray and meditate, but during the vacations a light took shape inside of me. I still loved Sadernac, and walked as much as I always had, but now I was bored by the blackberries and the hazelnuts of the hedges; I wanted to taste the milk of the wood-spurge, to bite into the poisonous berries the colour of red lead, which are enigmatically called Solomon's seal. I did all sorts of forbidden things. I ate apples between meals and snuck off with copies of Alexandre Dumas from the highest shelves in the library. I had instructive conversations about the mystery of childbirth with the tenant's daughter, and at night, in my bed, I told myself the strangest of stories which put me in the strangest of states. One night, sleeping in a damp field, looking up at the moon, I said to myself *these are sins!* And yet I was firmly resolved to continue to eat, read, talk and dream exactly as I pleased. I don't believe in God! I said to myself. How could I believe in God and deliberately decide to disobey Him? The truth of it stunned me for a moment: I didn't believe in God.

Papa didn't believe either, and neither did the writers I admired. Without God, the world no doubt was difficult to explain, but God didn't explain very much, or at any rate we understood very little. I took to this new state of affairs without much difficulty. However, when I returned to Paris, panic took hold of me. We can't help what we think, and yet Papa had once spoken of shooting the defeatists, and a year earlier, an older student had been (I had heard it whispered) kicked out of school because she had lost her faith. I was going to have to carefully conceal my disgrace; at night, I woke up sweating in fear that Andrée might suspect something.

Luckily, we never spoke of either sexuality or religion. We had plenty of other problems to occupy our attention.

We were studying the French Revolution; we admired Camille Desmoulins, Madame Roland and even Danton. We could lose ourselves for hours in discussions of property, justice and equality. We had zero respect for our teachers' opinions, and our parents' ideas didn't satisfy us either. My father voluntarily read *L'Action française*.[6] Monsieur Gallard was more of a democrat; in his youth he had been interested in Marc Sangnier; but he was no longer young, and he explained to Andrée that socialism necessarily resulted in the lowering of standards and the abolition of spiritual values.[7] He didn't convince us, but some of his arguments worried us. We tried to talk about things with Malou's friends, older girls who should have known much more than us, but they had similar ideas to Monsieur Gallard, and our questions didn't interest them. They preferred to discuss music, painting, literature, and stupidly for that matter. When she was entertaining, Malou often asked us to come and serve the tea, but she intuited that we didn't think very highly of her guests, and to get back at us she assumed an air of superiority over Andrée. One afternoon, Isabelle Barrière, who was in love, conveniently, with her piano teacher – a married man with three children – turned the conversation to romance novels; one by one, Malou, her cousin Guite and the Gosselin sisters indicated their favourites.

[6] A far-right, royalist newspaper (1908–1944).
[7] Marc Sangnier (1873–1950), a proponent of Catholic Socialism.

'What about you, Andrée?' asked Isabelle.

'Romance novels bore me,' said Andrée, as if she didn't want to hear any more about it.

'Now, now,' said Malou, 'we all know that you know *Tristan and Isolde* by heart.' She added that she didn't like this story, whereas Isabelle did; Isabelle declared that she found this epic of platonic love truly moving. Andrée burst out laughing.

'Platonic, Tristan and Isolde! No,' she said, 'there's nothing platonic about their love.'

There was an uncomfortable silence, and Guite said, in a prim voice, 'Little girls shouldn't speak about what they don't understand.'

Andrée laughed again, but didn't respond. I studied her face in confusion. What was it she was trying to say? I could only conceive of one kind of love: the love I had for her.

'Poor Isabelle!' said Andrée when we had retired to her room. 'She's going to have to get over her Tristan – she's nearly engaged to someone bald and awful.' She laughed. 'I hope she believes in love at first vow.'

'What's that?'

'My Aunt Louisa, Guite's mother, says that when two people take their wedding vows before the priest, they fall immediately in love. It's very convenient for mothers, this theory; it means they don't have to worry about their daughters' feelings. God will take care of that.'

'Nobody really believes that,' I said.

'Guite does.' Andrée was quiet for a moment. 'Maman doesn't go as far as all that,' she went on, 'but she says that once we're married, we are filled with grace.' She looked over at the portrait of her mother. 'Maman was very happy with Papa,' she said in an uncertain voice; 'and yet if Grand-mère hadn't forced her, she wouldn't have married him. She refused him twice.'

I looked at the photo of Madame Gallard. It was odd to think of her with a young girl's heart. 'She refused him!'

'Yes. Papa struck her as too stern. But he loved her, and he didn't lose heart. And once they were engaged she began to love him back.' Andrée sounded unconvinced.

For a moment we sat in silence.

'It must not be very amusing to live from morning to night with someone you don't love,' I said.

'It must be horrible,' said Andrée. She shivered, as if she had seen an orchid; gooseflesh stood out on her arms.

'They teach you in catechism to respect your body. So selling your body in marriage must be as bad as selling it on the street,' she said.

'No one is forced to get married,' I said.

'I will get married,' Andrée said. 'But not before I'm twenty-two.' She abruptly opened our Latin homework. 'Shall we get to work?'

I sat beside her, and we became absorbed in translating a text on the Battle of Trasimene.

We never served tea again to Malou and her friends. It was clear that whatever questions preoccupied us, we could only rely on ourselves to try to answer them. We never had more ardent conversations than we did that year. And despite the secret I kept from her, we were never closer. We were permitted to go to the Odéon theatre to see the classics. We discovered the Romantics: I was enraptured by Hugo, while Andrée preferred Musset, and we both admired Vigny. We began to make plans for the future. It was understood that after we'd finished secondary school I would continue my studies; Andrée also hoped to be allowed to attend classes at the Sorbonne. At the end of the trimester came the greatest joy of my childhood: Madame Gallard unexpectedly invited me to spend two weeks in Béthary, and Maman said I could go.

I thought that Andrée would be waiting for me at the station, but when I got off the train I was surprised to find Madame Gallard there instead. She wore a black and white dress, an enormous black straw hat decorated with daisies, and a white silk ribbon around her neck. She brought her lips to my forehead without quite touching it.

'Did you have a good trip, dear?'

'Very good, Madame, but I'm afraid I'm quite covered in coal dust.' In the presence of Madame Gallard, I always felt somehow guilty. My hands were dirty, and no doubt my face as well, but she didn't seem to notice; she had a distracted air. She smiled mechanically at the train staff and guided us to a cart hitched to a bay; she unwound the reins from a post and energetically hopped up onto the bench. 'Up you get.'

I climbed up next to her; she let the reins go loose between her gloved hands.

'I wanted to speak with you before you saw Andrée,' she said, without looking at me.

I tensed up. What kind of instruction was I about to receive? Had she guessed that I had lost my faith? But if so, why had she invited me to come?

'Andrée is having some difficulties, and you must help me.'

'Andrée is having some difficulties?' I repeated idiotically. It was disconcerting to be treated like a grown-up by Madame Gallard; there was something suspect about it. She pulled on the reins and clicked her tongue; the horse set off, with slow shuffling steps.

'Has Andrée ever spoken to you about her friend Bernard?'

'No.'

We were travelling down a dusty road, bordered by black locust trees. Madame Gallard went quiet.

'Bernard's father owns the property bordering my mother's,' she said, finally. 'He comes from one of those Basque families who made a fortune in Argentina; that's where he lives most of the year, with his wife and children. But Bernard was fragile and didn't do well in that climate; he spent his childhood here, with an elderly aunt and his private tutors.' Madame Gallard looked at me. 'After her accident Andrée spent a year in Béthary, bedridden. Bernard came every day to play with her. She was alone, and suffering, and bored, and given how young they were, I didn't concern myself about it,' she said, sounding guilty, though I didn't understand why.

'Andrée didn't tell me anything about it,' I said. My throat was tight. I wanted to jump out of the cart and run away, as I had run from Abbé Dominique's confessional that day.

'They saw each other every summer, they rode horses together. They were still only children. But then they grew up.' Madame Gallard tried to meet my gaze. There was an imploring look in her eyes. 'Sylvie, you have to understand: it is absolutely out of the question for Bernard and Andrée to marry. Bernard's father is as opposed to the idea as we are. So I had to order Andrée not to see him again.'

I stammered the first thing that came into my mind. 'I understand.'

'She took it very badly,' said Madame Gallard. Again she looked at me with that suspicious, supplicating look. 'All my hopes rest with you.'

'What can I do?' I asked. Words were coming out of my mouth, but they had no meaning. My ears were ringing.

'Distract her, talk to her about things that interest her. And, if the occasion presents itself, reason with her. I'm afraid she'll make herself sick. But there's nothing I can say to her just now,' she added.

She was visibly troubled and unhappy, but I didn't have any sympathy for her; on the contrary, just then, I hated her.

'I'll try,' I murmured, but I didn't mean it.

The horse trotted down an oak-lined avenue and came to a stop before a large house covered in ivy, which I recognised from the photograph on Andrée's mantelpiece. Now I understood why she loved Béthary and horse riding; now I knew what she was thinking of when her gaze grew distant.

'Hello!' Andrée smiled as she walked down the front steps to greet us; she wore a white dress with a green necklace, her short hair shining like a helmet; she seemed like a real young lady, and I suddenly realised that she was very pretty. It was an odd idea; we were so little interested in beauty.

'I think Sylvie would probably like to freshen up a bit, and then you can come down to dinner,' said Madame Gallard.

I followed Andrée through the entrance hall, which smelled of crème caramel and fresh wax, with a hint of old granary; turtle doves cooed; someone was playing the piano. We went up a flight of stairs and Andrée pushed open a door. 'Maman has put you in my room,' she said.

There was a large canopied bed with twisted bedposts, and on the other side of the room a narrow divan. How delighted I would have been only an hour before, to sleep in the same room as Andrée! But I stood there with a lump forming in my throat, wondering why Madame Gallard was making use of me. To win forgiveness? To distract Andrée? To spy on her? What exactly did she fear?

Andrée went to the window. 'When the weather is clear, you can see the Pyrénées,' she said with indifference.

Evening fell, and the weather was not clear. I got cleaned up and tidied my hair while unconvincingly recounting my journey. I had taken the train by myself for the first time, it had been a real adventure, but I found nothing else to say about it.

'You should cut your hair,' said Andrée.

'Maman doesn't want me to,' I said. Maman thought short hair made you look like the wrong sort of person. I pinned my hair into a limp chignon at my neck.

'Let's go downstairs, I want to show you the library,' said Andrée.

Whoever it was was still playing the piano, and some children were singing. The house was full of different sounds; the clanking of dishes being stacked, the echoes of footsteps. I went into the library and saw a complete collection of *La Revue des Deux Mondes*, starting from the very first issue, the works of Louis Veuillot and of

Montalembert, the sermons of Lacordaire, the speeches of the Comte de Mun, all of Joseph de Maistre.[8] On pedestal tables sat portraits of old men with beards and side whiskers: all Andrée's ancestors, and all fervent Catholics. Although they were dead, they seemed at home here, whereas among these austere gentlemen, Andrée seemed out of place: too young, too fragile, and above all, too alive.

A bell rang and we went into the dining room. There were so many of them! I knew them all, except the grandmother; under her white hair parted in the middle, and pulled back over each ear, she looked like a typical grandmother, and I didn't think much else of her. The older brother wore a cassock; he had just started at the seminary. He was having what seemed to be an ongoing conversation with Malou and Monsieur Gallard about women's suffrage. Yes, it was outrageous that a housewife should have more rights than a drunken labourer; but Monsieur Gallard's objection was that among the working classes,

[8] Louis Veuillot (1813–1883), a Catholic polemicist; Montalembert (1810–1870) was a theorist of Liberal Catholicism; Lacordaire (1802–1861) was a priest and a journalist who re-established the Dominican order after the French Revolution destroyed it; the Comte de Mun (1841–1914) was a prominent Catholic social reformer (as well as an anti-Dreyfusard and anti-Semite); Joseph de Maistre (1753–1821) was a moral philosopher who believed the rejection of Christianity was to blame for the bloodshed and chaos of the French Revolution.

the women were more radical than the men; if the law was passed, it would benefit the enemies of the Church. Andrée kept her mouth shut. At the other end of the table, the twins were throwing little balls of bread at each other; Madame Gallard looked on and only smiled. For the first time I realised that smile was a trap. I had often envied Andrée her independence, but suddenly she seemed much less free than I was. She had this past behind her, and around her, and this large house struck me as a care-fully guarded prison for the offspring of this enormous family.

'So?' asked Malou, rather harshly. 'What do you think of us?'

'Me? Nothing, why?'

'You've just looked at all of us around the table: you must be thinking something.'

'Only that there are so many of you, that's all,' I said. I told myself that I was going to have to learn how to keep my thoughts from showing on my face.

When dinner was over, Madame Gallard said to Andrée: 'You should show Sylvie the grounds.'

'Yes,' said Andrée.

'Take some coats, it's chilly outside.'

In the hallway Andrée took down a pair of loden capes. The turtle doves were sleeping. We went out through the back door, which gave onto the service quarters. Between the outhouse and the woodshed, a wolf-dog pulled on his chain and whined. Andrée went up to his kennel. 'Come on Mirza, poor thing, I'll take you for a walk.' She unhooked the creature, who leapt joyfully onto her and took off at full tilt ahead of us.

'Do you think that animals have a soul?' she asked me.

'I don't know.'

'If they don't, how unfair! They are as unhappy as people. And they don't understand why,' she added. 'It's worse when you don't understand.'

I didn't say anything. I had so been looking forward to this evening! I had thought I would finally be at the centre of Andrée's life, but never had she seemed so far away to me. She wasn't the same Andrée, now that her secret had a name. We walked silently through overgrown paths full of bluets and mallow. The park was full of beautiful trees and flowers.

'Let's sit down over there,' Andrée said, pointing to a bench beneath an Atlas cedar. She took a pack of Gauloises from her bag. 'Do you want one?'

'No,' I said. 'Since when do you smoke?'

'Maman doesn't let me, but once you've started disobeying ...' she lit up her cigarette and got smoke in her own eyes.

I gathered my courage. 'Andrée, what is going on? Tell me.'

'I expect Maman has already told you what's been happening,' she said. 'She was so insistent about fetching you from the train ...'

'She mentioned your friend Bernard. You never told me anything about him.'

'I couldn't tell you anything about Bernard,' she said, and her left hand opened and closed in a kind of spasm. 'Now it's public knowledge.'

'We don't have to talk about it if you don't want to,' I said quickly.

Andrée looked at me. 'You're different. You I want to tell.' With a bit of effort, she managed to inhale a bit of smoke. 'What did Maman tell you?'

'How you two became friends, and how she's forbidden you from seeing him again.'

'She has forbidden me,' said Andrée. She tossed her cigarette and ground it out with her heel. 'The night I got here, Bernard and I went for a walk after dinner. I got home late. Maman was waiting up for me; I saw right away that she had a funny look on her face. She asked me all these questions.' Andrée shrugged and said, in an irritated voice, 'She asked me if we had kissed each other! Of course we kiss each other, we're in love!'

I lowered my head. Andrée was unhappy and the idea of it was unbearable. But her unhappiness was so foreign to me; the kind of love where you kiss had no truth for me.

'Maman said horrible things to me,' Andrée said, tightening her loden cape around her body.

'But why?'

'His parents are much richer than us, but they don't move in our social circles, not at all. It seems that over in Rio, they lead an outlandish lifestyle, extravagant, really,' she said with a puritanical air. Then she added, under her breath, 'and Bernard's mother is Jewish.'

I watched Mirza, who lay without moving in the middle of the lawn, her ears pointed up towards the stars. I was no more capable than she was of expressing what I felt in words.

'And?' I asked.

'Maman went to speak to Bernard's father and they are in complete agreement: I am not a good match. He decided to bring Bernard to Biarritz for the holidays, and from there they'll leave for Argentina. Bernard is doing quite well now.'

'Has he already left?'

'Yes. Maman forbid me to say goodbye to him, but I did anyway. You can't imagine,' said Andrée. 'There is nothing so awful as making the person you love suffer.' Her voice trembled. 'He cried. How he cried!'

'How old is he?' I asked. 'What's he like?'

'He's fifteen, like me. But he doesn't know anything about the world. No one ever cared much about him, I was all he had.' She rummaged through her bag. 'I have a little photo of him.'

I looked at the little boy, this stranger who loved Andrée, who had kissed her, and who had cried so much.

He had large, light, heavy-lidded eyes, with short hair cut like a Roman emperor; he looked like Saint Tarcisius the martyr.

'He has the eyes and the cheeks of a little boy,' said Andrée, 'but look how sad his mouth is. He looks like he's apologising for having been born.' She leaned her head against the back of the bench and looked up at the sky. 'Sometimes, I think that I would rather he were dead. At least then I'd be the only one to suffer.' Her hand convulsed again. 'I can't bear the thought that at this very moment he might be crying.'

'You'll see each other again!' I said. 'Because you love each other, you'll see each other again. One day, when you're of age.'

'In six years? That's too far away. At our age that's much too far away. No,' said Andrée in despair, 'I know very well that I will never see him again.'

Never. The word had never fallen with such weight upon my heart. I repeated it within myself, under the never-ending sky, and I wanted to cry.

'When I came back from saying goodbye to him, I climbed up on the roof of the house. I wanted to jump.'

'You wanted to kill yourself?'

'I stayed up there for two hours; for two hours I hesitated. I told myself that I didn't care if my soul was damned; if God wasn't good, I didn't care about going to His heaven.' She shrugged. 'But I was scared anyway. Not scared of dying – on the contrary, I wanted so much to be dead! But scared of hell. If I go to hell, it's for eternity, and I'll never see Bernard again.'

'You will see him again in this life!' I said.

Andrée shook her head. 'It's over.' She suddenly got up. 'Let's go back. I'm cold.'

We walked across the lawn in silence. Andrée chained up Mirza and we went up to our room. I slept in the canopy bed, and Andrée on the divan. She turned out the light.

'I didn't tell Maman that I saw Bernard again,' she said. 'I didn't want to hear the things she would say.'

I hesitated. I didn't care for Madame Gallard, but I owed Andrée the truth. 'She's very worried about you,' I said.

'Yes, I suppose she is worried,' said Andrée.

★★★

Andrée didn't mention Bernard in the days that followed, and I didn't dare bring him up. In the mornings, she played the violin, and almost always something sad. Then we went out into the sun. This part of the country was drier than mine; I learned through our long dusty walks the rough scent of fig trees; in the forest I grew to know the taste of pine nuts, and licked the resinous tears solidified on the trunks of the trees that shed them. When we came back from our walks, Andrée went to the stables and caressed her small chestnut horse, but she never mounted him anymore.

Our afternoons were less peaceful. Madame Gallard had decided it was time to marry off Malou, and to camouflage the visits of these more or less unknown young suitors, she opened the house to visits from all the 'decent' people in the neighbourhood. We played croquet and tennis, and danced on the lawn; we talked about rain and good weather while eating teacakes. The day Malou came down from her room in a dress of raw shantung silk, her hair freshly washed and set with the curling iron, Andrée elbowed me. 'She's dressed like a debutante.'

Malou spent that afternoon beside a dreadful student from the military school at Saint-Cyr, who didn't play tennis, who didn't dance, who didn't speak; from time to time he ran after our balls. When he left, Madame Gallard shut herself in the library with her eldest daughter; the window was open and we could hear Malou's voice protesting, 'No Maman, not him, he's far too boring!'

'Poor Malou!' said Andrée. 'All the ones they introduce to her are so stupid and ugly!' She sat on the swing. Next to the outhouse was a kind of outdoor gymnasium; Andrée often exercised on the trapeze or the pull-up bar; she was very strong. She grabbed the ropes. 'Push me.'

I pushed her. When she had a bit of momentum, she stood on the seat and gave it a vigorous jerk with her knees. Soon the swing was arching up towards the tops of the trees. 'Not so high!' I cried out.

She didn't answer; she flew up, fell back and flew ever higher upwards. The twins, who had been playing with sawdust in the shed, next to the doghouse, looked up with interest; in the distance could be heard the flat sound of rackets hitting balls. Andrée brushed past the leaves of the maple trees, and I began to be afraid; I heard the steel hooks beginning to creak. 'Andrée!'

The whole house was quiet; from the basement window came the distant sounds of the kitchen; the delphiniums and the honesties bordering the wall barely moved. But I was afraid. I didn't dare seize the seat of the swing, or beg her too strongly, but I thought that the swing was going to go over or that Andrée would be overcome with dizziness and let go of the ropes; just watching her swing back and forth up into the sky like a pendulum gone mad was making me nauseous. Why did she keep at it for so long? She passed by me, standing straight up in her white dress, her eyes were motionless, her lips pressed together. Maybe something had broken inside her mind, and she couldn't stop. The dinner bell rang and Mirza began to howl. Andrée went on flying up into the trees. 'She's going to kill herself,' I thought.

'Andrée!' Someone else had shouted her name. Madame Gallard was striding towards us, her face dark with anger. 'Come down from there at once! That's an order! Get down!'

Andrée blinked and looked down towards the ground; she squatted, sat and braked with her feet so abruptly that it laid her out on the grass.

'Did you hurt yourself?'

'No.' She started to laugh, which turned to hiccups, and she lay there on the ground, her eyes closed.

'You've clearly made yourself sick! Half an hour on the swing! How old do you think you are?' said Madame Gallard in a hard voice.

Andrée opened her eyes. 'The sky is spinning.'

'You have to make a cake for tea tomorrow.'

'I'll do it after dinner,' said Andrée, getting up. She put her hand on my shoulder. 'I'm reeling.'

Madame Gallard went off again; she took the twins by the hand and led them back to the house. Andrée lifted her head and looked up at the treetops. 'It's nice up there.'

'You scared me,' I said.

'Oh, the swing's pretty solid, no one's ever had an accident,' Andrée said.

No, she hadn't wanted to kill herself, all that was behind her, but when I remembered the way she stared and tightened her mouth, I was afraid.

After dinner, when the kitchen was empty, Andrée and I went down there. It was an enormous room which took up half of the basement; during the day you could see through the basement window a constant parade of pig haunches, guinea fowl and dogs, and human feet, but at this hour nothing else stirred, except for Mirza, tied up and whining faintly. The fire roared in the cast-iron stove; there was no other sound. While Andrée cracked eggs and measured sugar and yeast, I inspected the walls and rifled through the sideboard. There were piles of shiny copper pots and pans, skimming ladles, basins, bed-warmers that had once heated the beds of those bearded ancestors; on the credenza I admired the slew of childishly coloured enamel plates. Everything was made of cast iron, earthenware, stoneware, porcelain, tin, aluminium; there were cooking pots, frying pans, saucepans, skillets, cauldrons, casseroles, soup bowls, serving platters, tureens, tumblers, colanders, mincers, mills, moulds and mortars. An endless variety of bowls, cups, glasses, champagne flutes and coupes, plates, saucers, sauce boats, jars, jugs, pitchers, carafes. Does each kind of spoon, ladle, fork and knife really have its own particular purpose? Do we really have so many different needs to satisfy? This clandestine subterranean world must turn up on the surface of the earth for enormous and discerning dinner parties that I knew nothing about.

'Do you really use everything?' I asked Andrée.

'More or less. There are so many traditions,' she answered. She put the pale unbaked cake in the oven. 'You haven't seen anything yet. Let's go look at the wine cellar.'

We had to pass through the dairy. Earthenware jugs, glazed ceramic bowls, polished wooden butter churns, clumps of butter, silky-fleshed fromage blanc under white muslin; all that exposed food, and the milky newborn smell of it, made me want to flee. I preferred the cellars full of dusty bottles and little casks swollen with alcohol, but I felt oppressed by all that ham and cured meat, those heaps of onions and potatoes. Now I understand why she needs to go flying through the trees, I thought, looking at Andrée.

'Do you like cherries soaked in eau de vie?'

'I've never tried it.'

On a shelf, there were hundreds of jars of jam, each covered with parchment paper on which it was noted when it was made and what kind of fruit it contained. There were also jars of fruit conserved in syrup and alcohol. Andrée took a cherry one, which she brought to the kitchen. She placed it on the table. With a little wooden ladle, she filled two goblets, and sipped the pink liquid. 'Grand-mère didn't hold back on the alcohol,' she said. 'A girl could get herself drunk on that!'

I picked one up by its stem; the fruit looked wilted, all wrinkled and discoloured. It didn't taste like a cherry anymore, but I liked the warmth of the alcohol. 'Have you ever been drunk?' I asked her.

Her face lit up. 'Once, with Bernard. We drank a flask of Chartreuse. At first it was fun; I was even dizzier than when I got off the swing, but afterward, we were sick to our stomachs.'

The fire flared, and we began to smell the soft odour of something baking. Since Andrée had brought up Bernard, I felt emboldened to ask about him.

'You became friends after your accident? Did he come to see you often?'

'Yes. We played draughts, dominoes, crapette. Bernard would fly into terrible rages back then; one time, I accused him of having cheated and he kicked me, right in my injured thigh. He didn't do it on purpose, but I fainted from the pain. When I came to, he had called for help, they were redoing my bandages and he was at my bedside in tears.' Andrée looked away. 'I had never seen a little boy cry. My brother and cousin are brutes. When they left us alone, we would kiss ...' She refilled our goblets; the smell intensified as the cake browned in the oven. Mirza was no longer whining; she must have been asleep. Everyone was asleep.

'He fell in love with me,' said Andrée. She turned to look at me. 'I can't explain it – it made such a change in my life. I had always thought that no one could love me.'

'Did you really think that?' I asked, startled.

'Yes.'

'But why?'

She shrugged. 'I thought I was so ugly, so clumsy and uninteresting; nobody really cared about me.'

'What about your mother?'

'Oh, well. A mother has to love her children, that doesn't count. Maman loved us all, and there were so many of us!' There was disgust in her voice. Had she been jealous of her brothers and sisters? Had she suffered from the coldness I felt emanating from Madame Gallard? I had never thought that Andrée's love for her mother could be an unhappy one. She pressed her hands against the gleaming wood of the table.

'Bernard was the only person in the world who loved me for myself, exactly as I was, and because I was myself,' she said fiercely.

'What about me?' I asked. The words had just fallen out of my mouth; I was revolted by how unjust it all was.

Andrée stared at me in surprise. 'You?'

'Didn't I value you for who you were?'

'Of course,' Andrée said in an uncertain voice.

The warmth of the alcohol and my indignation made me brave. I wanted to say to Andrée the kinds of things you only say in books.

'You never knew it, but from the day I met you, you were everything to me,' I said. 'I had decided that if you died, I would immediately die as well.' I spoke in the past tense, and tried to make my voice sound detached. Andrée continued to look at me, perplexed.

'I thought your books and your studies were all that was really important to you,' she said.

'You were more important. I would have given anything to keep from losing you.'

She didn't say anything.

'Did you not suspect it?'

'When you gave me that bag for my birthday, I thought that you felt truly affectionate towards me.'

'It was so much more than that!' I said, sadly.

She looked moved. How had I failed to make her feel that I loved her? She had appeared so glorious to me that I had assumed she had everything she wanted. I wanted to cry for her, and for myself.

'How odd,' Andrée said. 'We were inseparable for so many years, and yet I realise I didn't really know you! I form opinions of people too quickly,' she said with remorse.

I didn't want her to blame herself. 'I didn't really know you either,' I said vigorously. 'I thought you were proud to be as you were. I envied you.'

'I am not proud,' she said. She got up and walked over to the stove. 'The cake is ready,' she said, opening the oven. She blew out the flame, and put the cake away in a cupboard. We went up to her room, and while we were undressing she asked: 'Will you take Communion tomorrow morning?'

'No,' I said.

'Then let's go to Mass together. I won't take Communion either. I'm in a state of sin,' she said indifferently. 'I still haven't told Maman I disobeyed her, and what's worse, I'm not sorry I did.'

I slipped into the sheets, between the twisted bed-posts. 'You couldn't let Bernard leave without seeing him again.'

'I couldn't!' Andrée said. 'He would have thought I didn't care, and he would have despaired even more. I couldn't,' she repeated.

'Well, then you were right to disobey,' I said.

'Oh,' said Andrée, 'sometimes no matter what you do, it's bad.'

She made as if to go to sleep, but left the little blue lamp lit on her bedside table.

'That's something that puzzles me,' she said. 'Why doesn't God tell us clearly what he wants from us?'

I didn't answer.

Andrée shifted in her bed, and rearranged her pillows.

'I want to ask you something.'

'Go on.'

'Do you still believe in God?'

I didn't hesitate. Tonight, the truth didn't frighten me. 'No, I don't believe. For the last year I haven't.'

'I thought as much,' said Andrée.

She propped herself up on her pillows.

'Sylvie! There can't just be this life!'

'I don't believe in God,' I repeated.

'Sometimes it's very difficult,' said Andrée. 'Why does God want us to be unhappy? My brother tells me that it has to do with the question of Evil, and that the Fathers of the Church resolved it long ago. He tells me what they tell him at the seminary, but it doesn't satisfy me.'

'No,' I said. 'If God exists there's no explanation for Evil.'

'But perhaps we have to accept that we don't understand,' said Andrée. 'It's prideful to want to understand everything.' She put out the light and added, quietly, 'There must be another life. There has to be another life!'

I don't know what exactly I expected when I woke up the next morning, but I felt deflated. Andrée was the same. I was the same. We said good morning the way we always had. My disappointment lingered over the following days. Of course, we were very close, we couldn't be any closer; after six years of friendship one short conversation doesn't mean very much. But when I thought back to what we'd talked about in the kitchen, I was sad to think that in reality, nothing had changed.

One morning, we were sitting beneath a fig tree, eating its fruit. The purple ones you get in Paris are stupid and tasteless; I loved these small pale green ones, filled with grainy jam.

'I spoke with Maman last night,' said Andrée.

I felt a pinch in my heart. Andrée always seemed closer to me the further she was from her mother.

'She asked if I would take Communion on Sunday. She was greatly troubled by the fact that I didn't take Communion last week.'

'Did she guess the reason?'

'Not exactly. But I told her anyway.'

'You told her!'

Andrée pressed the fig against her cheek. 'Poor Maman. She has so many troubles just now, because of Malou and also because of me!'

'Did she punish you?'

'She told me that as far as she was concerned, she forgave me, but beyond that it is between me and my confessor.'

Andrée looked at me, her face grave.

'You have to understand her,' she said. 'She's meant to look after my soul. She must not know either what God expects of her. It's not easy for anyone.'

'No, it isn't easy,' I said vaguely. I was furious. Madame Gallard was torturing Andrée, but somehow she was the victim?

'The way she spoke to me really affected me,' Andrée said with emotion in her voice. 'You know, she also went through some difficulties when she was young.' She looked around us. 'Right here, in these very paths, she had some difficult times.'

'Was your grandmother very strict?'

'Yes.'

Andrée thought for a moment. 'Maman says there is such a thing as grace, that God knows how great are the tests He sends us, that He will help Bernard and that He will help me as He helped her.'

She tried to meet my eye. 'Sylvie, if you don't believe in God, how can you bear to be alive?'

'But I love being alive,' I said.

'So do I. But that's just it; if I thought that the people I loved would die and that would be the end of them, I would kill myself immediately.'

'I don't want to kill myself,' I said.

We left the shade of the fig tree and walked back to the house in silence. Andrée took Communion that Sunday.

PART TWO

We passed the baccalaureate exam, and after much debate, Madame Gallard finally gave her consent: Andrée could attend the Sorbonne for three years. Andrée chose to study literature, while I opted for philosophy; we often studied side by side at the library, but in class I found myself alone. The way the other students talked, or acted, the declarations they made, alarmed me; I continued to respect Christian morality, and they seemed a bit too liberated to me. It was no accident that I found I had much in common with Pascal Blondel, who was reputed to be an observant Catholic. I was as attracted to his impeccable manners and his beautiful angelic face as I was to his intelligence. He smiled at his classmates but kept them at a distance, and seemed to be particularly wary of female students, but my philosophical zeal won out over his reserve. We had endless lofty conversations, and when all was said and done, apart from the existence of God, we agreed about nearly everything else.

Pascal detested public places, libraries and bistros, so I went to study at his house. He lived with his father and sister, in an apartment much like our own; I was disappointed by how ordinary his bedroom was. Coming from my school, I found other young people to be a mysterious brotherhood, already versed in the secret elements of life, unlike me. But Pascal's furniture, his books, his ivory crucifix and his reproduction of a Greco painting showed that he was no different from me, or from Andrée. For a long time he had enjoyed the right to go out alone in the evenings and to read whatever he liked, but I soon saw that our horizons were similarly limited. He had been raised in a religious institution where his father taught, and cared only for his studies and his family. All I wanted was to move out of the family home, and it astonished me that he was so comfortable in his own. He would shake his head, saying 'I will never be happier than I am now' in the nostalgic tone of a much older man, longing for his youth. He told me that his father was a remarkable person. He had married late, after a difficult youth, and found himself a widower at fifty, with a ten-year-old daughter and a baby who was only a few months old; he had devoted himself entirely to them. As far as his sister was concerned, Pascal considered her a saint. She had lost her fiancé during the war, and had decided she would never marry. She wore her chestnut hair away from her face, gathered in a chignon, revealing a large and intimidating forehead. She had a pale complexion, soulful eyes, and a hard, barking laugh; she wore dark-coloured dresses, always tailored in the same elegantly austere style, with large white collars. She oversaw her brother's education, and had tried to steer him towards the priesthood. I suspected her of keeping a journal and of fancying herself Eugénie de Guérin.[9] While darning the family socks with her ruddy thick hands, she must have recited Verlaine: 'a humble life, with boring and easy chores'. Good son, good Christian, good student – Pascal was a little too good, I found; he sometimes resembled a seminary student. And a few of my characteristics irritated him right back. Nevertheless, even years later when I had much more interesting friends, our friendship remained strong. He was my escort the day the Gallards celebrated Malou's engagement.

In dutifully circling Napoleon's grave, sniffing the roses in the Parc de Bagatelle, and daintily ingesting Russian salad in Landais forests, Malou – who at that time knew all the words to *Carmen*, *Manon* and *Lakmé* – finally managed to find herself a husband. Ever since she'd turned

[9] Eugénie de Guérin (1805–1848) was a pious French author, the devoted elder sister of the poet Maurice de Guérin. She assiduously kept a journal addressed to her brother, who died at the age of twenty-eight.

twenty-five, her mother had been hounding her: 'Join a convent or get a husband; remaining unmarried is not a vocation.' One evening, as they were leaving for the opera, Madame Gallard declared: 'This is your final chance, take it or leave it; next time I'm taking Andrée.' It was then that Malou agreed to marry a forty-year-old widower who was saddled with two daughters. A morning dance had been organised to celebrate. Andrée insisted I come. I put on a grey silk jersey dress bequeathed me by a cousin who'd just entered a convent, and went to meet Pascal in front of the Gallards' house.

Monsieur Gallard had really come up in the world over the last five years, and now they lived in a luxurious apartment in the rue Marbeuf. I hardly ever set foot there. Madame Gallard reluctantly greeted me; it had been a long time since she had kissed my cheek when we met, and she no longer took the trouble even to smile at me. Pascal, however, received an unambiguously warm greeting; women in general responded well to him, because of the intense yet reserved way he had about him. Andrée gave him one of her standard smiles; she had shadows under her eyes, and I wondered if she had been crying. 'If you want to powder your nose, you'll find everything you need in my room,' she said; it was a discreet hint. In the Gallard house, face powder was allowed, whereas my mother and her sisters and friends looked down on it. 'Make-up ruins your complexion,' they said. My sisters and I often said to each other that given the state of their complexions, prudence hadn't exactly paid off.

I ran a little puff over my face, touched up my artlessly styled hair, and came back to the drawing room. The young people were dancing while the older women looked on sentimentally. It was not an attractive sight. Everyone wore colours that were too bright or too sweet, awkwardly cut dresses of taffeta and satin that bared their shoulders yet did not flatter these young Christian girls, who in any case had been raised to forget their bodies. Only Andrée was agreeable to look at, with her shiny hair and buffed nails, her pretty dark-blue dress and dainty high heels. But despite the healthy glow she had created through her make-up, she seemed tired.

'It's so sad!' I said to Pascal.

'What is?'

'All this!'

'No it's not!' he said, gaily. Pascal did not share my severity or my rare enthusiasms; he said there's something to love in everyone, and that's why people liked him: everyone felt lovable when he looked at them.

He asked me to dance, and then I danced with other boys. They were all ugly; I had nothing to say to them nor they to me; it was hot; I was bored. I kept an eye on Andrée. She smiled equitably at each of her dance partners, and curtsied to the older ladies a little too perfectly. I didn't like seeing her so easily fulfil her role of the young society girl. Would she let herself be married off, like her sister? I wondered, slightly anxious. A few months earlier, Andrée had run into Bernard in Biarritz. He was behind the wheel of a long, pale blue car, wearing a white three-piece suit and some rings; sat beside him was a pretty blonde who was clearly of easy virtue. They had shaken hands without finding anything to say to each other. 'Maman was right: we weren't a suitable match,' Andrée had told me. Maybe things would have been different if they hadn't been separated, I thought, or maybe not. In any case, since this meeting Andrée had only spoken of love with bitterness.

Between two dances I managed to take her aside. 'Could we possibly speak for a few minutes?'

She touched her temple; she likely had a headache, she had a lot of them in those days. 'Meet me on the stairs, top floor. I'll arrange to slip away.' She glanced at the dance floor, where people were beginning to recouple. 'Our mothers won't let us go walking with young men, but look at them laugh as we dance with them, they're so innocent!'

Sometimes Andrée crudely said out loud the kinds of things I could barely articulate even to myself. Yes, these good Christian women ought to be concerned seeing their daughters modest and flushed, losing themselves between masculine arms. How I had hated dancing lessons when I was fifteen! I experienced an indefinable malady, something like an uneasy stomach, or like fatigue, or sadness, and I didn't understand why; since I had learned the meaning of it, I had become resistant to dancing. It struck me as irrational and vexing that anyone who cared to could, merely by touching me, weaken my scruples. But there was no question that most of these young virgins were more naïve than I was, or less prideful. Now that I thought about it, it pained me to watch them. And what about Andrée? Her cynicism had often made me ask myself questions that scandalised me the minute I formulated them.

Andrée joined me on the stairs and we sat down on the highest step. 'It's good to catch my breath!' she said.

'Does your head hurt?'

'Yes.' She smiled. 'Maybe it's because of the little cocktail I made myself this morning. Usually, to get myself going, I drink some coffee or a glass of white wine; today I mixed the two.'

'Coffee and wine together?'

'It wasn't completely terrible. It was a real pick-me-up.' Andrée stopped smiling. 'I didn't sleep all night. I'm so sad for Malou!' Andrée had never got on very well with her sister, but she took people's misfortunes to heart. 'Poor Malou!' she said. 'For two days, she went running to consult each of her friends. Everyone told her to accept him. Especially Guite.' Andrée snickered. 'Guite says when you're twenty-eight years old it's intolerable to spend your nights alone!'

'And spending them with a man one doesn't love, is that more tolerable?' I smiled. 'Does Guite still believe in love at first vow?'

'I suppose,' said Andrée. She played nervously with the gold chain around her neck, from which hung her religious medallions. 'Well. It's not that simple. You – you'll have a career, you can be good for something without getting married. But a useless old spinster like Guite? Not very good,' she said.

I often congratulated myself, egoistically, that the Bolsheviks and bad luck had ruined my father; I was obliged to go out and work; the problems that tormented Andrée didn't concern me.

'Have they really forbidden you to sit the *agrégation*?'[10]

'It's impossible. Next year, this will be my party.'

'Your mother is really going to try to marry you off?'

Andrée snorted. 'I think she's already at it – there's a little *polytechnicien* who keeps asking me what kind of

[10] A competitive and prestigious exam which allowed university graduates to teach secondary school. Simone de Beauvoir passed hers in philosophy in 1929, second only to Sartre; some have suggested their scores were negligibly close, but the jury decided they couldn't allow a woman to come in first. In recent years, *Mémoires d'une jeune fille rangée* has often been set as a text for the French literature *agrégation*.

things I like. I told him I dreamed of caviar, couture and nightclubs, and that my ideal man was Louis Jouvet.[11]

'Did he believe you?'

'In any case he seemed worried.'

We chatted a few minutes more, and then Andrée looked at her watch.

'I have to go back down.'

It was like a little gold manacle. I hated it. When we read by the tranquil light of the green lamps at the library, when we drank tea in the rue Soufflot, when we walked in the Luxembourg Gardens, Andrée often glanced at her watch, and if she were running late, would take off in a panic. She always had something she had to do; her mother piled on the chores, and she accomplished them with the zeal of the truly penitent. She doted on her mother, but if she disobeyed in some respects, it was her mother's own fault. Not long after my visit to Béthary, when Andrée was only fifteen, Madame Gallard made her aware of the mechanics of love in such minute detail that when Andrée thought back to their conversation she shivered. Afterward her mother calmly allowed her to read Lucretius, Boccaccio and Rabelais; Madame Gallard was such a good Christian

[11] Louis Jouvet (1887–1951) was an actor and theatre director, a founding member of the avant-garde Cartel company which the girls go to see a few pages later.

that these crude, obscene works didn't worry her, but she irredeemably condemned those she accused of misrepresenting Catholic belief and morality. If she caught Andrée reading Claudel, Mauriac or Bernanos, she would tell her to read 'the Fathers of the Church'. She believed that I was a pernicious influence on Andrée, and she had tried to forbid her from seeing me. With the support of an open-minded advisor, Andrée had held her ground. But as a way of asking forgiveness for studying, going to lectures, continuing our friendship, she devoted herself to assiduously and irreproachably carrying out what Madame Gallard called her social duties. This is why she so often had a headache; during the daytime, she barely found the time to practise her violin; nights she reserved to studying but though her courses didn't give her too much difficulty, she wasn't getting enough sleep.

Pascal danced with her quite a bit towards the end of the day. As he was walking me home, he said, with great earnestness, 'Your friend is lovely. I've often seen you at the Sorbonne together – why have you never introduced us?'

'It didn't occur to me,' I said.

'I would like to see her again.'

'That's easy enough.'

I was surprised that he was so susceptible to Andrée's charms; he was friendly with women, as he was with men, or perhaps a little more, but he didn't seem to have much time for them. In spite of his universal kindness, he didn't easily form attachments. As for Andrée, behind her new façade she still tended to be mistrustful. As she'd grown up, she had been outraged to discover the chasm which lay between the teachings of the gospels and the self-centred, egotistical and petty conduct of those who professed to live according to them. She kept their hypocrisy at bay with a healthy dose of cynicism. She believed me when I said that Pascal was very bright, but though she loathed stupidity, she didn't much value intelligence. 'What good is it?' she asked with a kind of irritation. I don't know what exactly she wanted, but all recognised values were met with the same scepticism where Andrée was concerned. If she became besotted with an artist, or a writer, or an actor, it was always for the most unexpected reasons; she liked them for their more frivolous, or even dubious, qualities. Jouvet had so charmed her in the role of a drunkard that she hung his picture in her bedroom; these infatuations were a means of challenging the false virtues of 'decent' people; she didn't set much store by them. But she seemed serious when she said that she found Pascal to be 'very nice'.

And so Pascal came for tea with us in the rue Soufflot, and walked with us to the Luxembourg. The second time, I left him alone with Andrée, and after that they often took to meeting up without me. I wasn't jealous. Since that night in the kitchen at Béthary, when I had confessed to Andrée how much she meant to me, I had begun to let go of her a little. She was still enormously important to me, but now the rest of the world was opening up to me; she was no longer everything.

Madame Gallard, reassured to see Andrée's studies completed without having cost her either her faith or her values, and satisfied with seeing her eldest daughter settled, demonstrated a certain amount of liberalism that spring. Andrée looked at her watch much less frequently; she often saw Pascal alone, or we went out all three of us together. And he began to have some influence over her. From the outset he laughed at her acerbic observations, her jaded witticisms, but soon he began to reproach her pessimism. 'Human nature is not so dark,' he told her. They discussed the problem of evil, sin and grace, and he accused Andrée of Jansenism. She was truly struck by him. The first few times, she said, 'He's so young!' Then she said, in a bewildered tone, 'When I compare myself to Pascal, I feel like I'm an old, embittered spinster.' And in the end he convinced her. 'Having preconceived negative thoughts about one's peers is an offense to God,' she said. She also said: 'A Christian should have standards, but not be tormented by them,' adding, enthusiastically, 'Pascal is the first real Christian I've met!'

More than his arguments, it was Pascal's very existence that reconciled Andrée with human nature, with the world, with God. He believed in heaven, and he loved life; he was joyful, and he was irreproachable; so all men were not bad, then, nor all virtues false; and paradise could be attained without renouncing life on earth. I praised Andrée for letting herself be persuaded. Two years earlier, her faith had seemed to waver: 'There is only one possible faith,' she told me then; 'and it's that of the coalman.' Since then, her ideas had evolved; all I could hope was that she didn't turn religion into too cruel of an idea. Pascal, who shared her convictions, was in a better position than I was to reassure her that it wasn't a crime to sometimes look after herself. Without condemning Madame Gallard, he reassured Andrée that she had been right to stand up for her individuality. 'God doesn't want us to dull our wits; if He's given us certain gifts, it's because He wants us to make use of them,' he told her again and again. Hearing this, Andrée lit up; it was as if an enormous weight had been lifted from her shoulders. While the chestnut trees of the Luxembourg Gardens budded, leafed and bloomed, I saw her, too, transformed. In her flannel suit, straw cloche and gloves, she had the restrained allure of a young lady of breeding. Pascal joked with her light-heartedly. 'Why do you always wear hats that hide your face? Why do you never take off your gloves? May one invite such a well-behaved young person to sit on the terrace of a café?'

She seemed happy when he teased her. She didn't buy a new hat, but she left her gloves at the bottom of her bag, and sat on the terraces of the Boulevard Saint-Michel; a kind of a bounce came into her step that I hadn't seen since the days when we walked beneath the pine trees.

Previously, Andrée's beauty had been a kind of secret: it lived deep in her eyes, or sometimes flashed across her face, never completely visible. But suddenly it flowered on the surface of her skin, it erupted into daylight. I see her again, one verdantly scented morning, on the lake in the Bois de Boulogne. She had taken the oars. Hatless, gloveless and bare-armed, she glided dexterously over the water. Her hair shone. Her eyes shone. Pascal trailed a hand in the water and sang quietly; he had a lovely voice and he knew a lot of songs.

He, too, was changing. In the company of his father and sister, he had struck me as being like a little boy; but he spoke to Andrée with a man's authority. It wasn't that he was playing a role; it was that, quite simply, he had risen to the level of what she needed from him. Either I had misread him, or he was maturing. In any case, he seemed less like a seminary student, less angelic and more gay, and his gaiety suited him. On the afternoon of the 1st of May, he waited for us on the terrace of the Luxembourg; when he saw us, he climbed up onto the railing and walked gingerly over to meet us, like a tightrope walker, his arms out for balance. In each hand he held a bouquet of lily of the valley.[12] He jumped down and handed one to each of

---

[12] The 1st of May is the workers' holiday. Since the sixteenth century it has been the custom to offer sprigs of lily of the valley to symbolise the return of spring.

us. Mine was only for the sake of symmetry; Pascal had never given me flowers. Andrée understood, and her cheeks reddened; it was only the second time in our lives that I'd seen her blush. *They're in love*, I thought. Andrée did not give her affections easily: it was a great honour to be loved by her. But I was especially glad for her. She wouldn't have been able to marry a non-believer; if she had resigned herself to marry an austere Christian man like her father, she would have wasted away. With Pascal, she could finally reconcile duty and happiness.

It was the end of the year and we didn't have much work to do, so we wandered the city. None of the three of us was rich. Madame Gallard only gave her daughters enough pocket money to take the bus and buy stockings. Pascal wasn't permitted to earn anything as a tutor because Monsieur Blondel wanted him to focus exclusively on his exams; his father chose instead to break his back working overtime. I only had two students of my own, who paid badly. However, we still managed to go to the Studio des Ursulines to see abstract films, and avant-garde theatre performed by the Cartel.[13] Afterward Andrée and I always had long conversations about what we'd seen, while Pascal

[13] That is, an association of four directors (Louis Jouvet, Charles Dullin, Gaston Baty and Georges Pitoëff) founded in 1927 with the intention of giving avant-garde theatre the same visibility as more mainstream boulevard theatre.

listened to us indulgently. He admitted that he only loved philosophy; on their own, art and literature bored him, but when they purported to represent life, he said they rang false. He said that in reality, feelings and situations are never as subtle or as dramatic as they are in books. Andrée found this kind of commitment to simplicity refreshing. And since she was only too prone to see the world as tragic, she was better off with someone like Pascal whose wisdom was limited, but happy.

After passing her oral exams brilliantly, Andrée went for a walk with Pascal. He never invited her to his house, and doubtless if he had she wouldn't have accepted; she said vaguely to her mother that she was going out with me and some classmates but she didn't want to either admit to her or hide from her that she had spent the afternoon at the home of a young man. They always saw each other out of doors, and spent a lot of time walking. I met her the following day at our usual place, under the dead gaze of a stone queen. I had bought some cherries, the large black ones that she loved, but she refused to taste them; something seemed to be bothering her. After a moment, she said: 'I told Pascal about what happened with Bernard.' Her voice was tense.

'You hadn't ever told him?'

'No. For a long time I wanted to. I felt that I should, but I didn't dare to.' She hesitated. 'I was afraid he would judge me for it.'

'What an idea!' I said. It mattered little that I had known Andrée for ten years; she still managed, often, to perplex me.

'We never did anything bad, Bernard and I,' she said in a serious voice, 'but we did kiss and not platonically. Pascal is so pure. I was afraid he would be terribly shocked.' She added, with conviction, 'But he's only severe as far as he himself is concerned.'

'How could he have been shocked? You were children, you and Bernard, and you loved each other.'

'One can sin at any age,' Andrée said; 'and love isn't an excuse for everything.'

'Pascal must have thought you sounded like a Jansenist!' I said. I didn't understand her scruples; I also didn't really know what those childish kisses had meant to her.

'He understood,' she said. 'He always understands.' She looked around. 'And to think that I wanted to kill myself when Maman separated me from Bernard – I was so sure I would always love him!' An anxious note of interrogation crept into her voice.

'It's normal to get things wrong when you're fifteen,' I said.

With the toe of her shoe, Andrée traced lines in the gravel. 'How old do you have to be to think: this is forever?' Her face hardened when she was worried; it seemed almost skeletal.

'You're not getting it wrong now,' I said.

'I think you're right,' she said. She continued to trace uncertain lines on the ground. 'But what about him? How do you know the person you love will love you forever?'

'You must feel it,' I said.

She plunged her hand into the paper bag and silently ate a few cherries. 'Pascal told me that before now he never loved anyone,' Andrée said. She sought my gaze. 'He didn't say "I have never been in love"; he said "I have never loved."'

I smiled. 'Pascal is very precise; he chooses his words carefully.'

'He asked if we could take Communion together tomorrow morning.'

I didn't answer. I thought that if I had been in Andrée's position, I would have been jealous seeing Pascal take Communion. A human creature is such a small entity compared to God. But it's true that at one time, I had loved both Andrée and God with ferocity.

From then on, it was understood between the two of us that Andrée loved Pascal. As for him, he spoke to her with more confidence than he had in the past. He told her that between the ages of sixteen and eighteen he had wanted to be a priest; his advisor showed him that he didn't really have the calling for it. His sister had influenced him, and then, too, the seminary had been a refuge against modernity, and the adult responsibilities that frightened him. This apprehension hadn't gone away, and it explained why Pascal was biased where women were concerned. At the moment, he severely reproached himself for it. 'Purity is not a question of seeing the devil in every woman,' he said, with lightness in his voice, to Andrée. Before meeting her, he only made an exception for his sister, whom he considered to be a pure spirit, and for me, because I had so little awareness of being female. He understood now that women were, as women, God's creatures. 'However, there is only one Andrée in the world,' he added, with so much warmth that Andrée no longer had any doubt that he loved her.

'Will you write to each other over the holidays?' I asked.

'Yes.'

'What will your mother say?'

'Maman never opens my letters,' Andrée said, 'and she has better things to do than to watch over the post.'

This summer would be a particularly busy one, due to Malou's upcoming engagement party. Andrée was apprehensive about it. 'Would you come if Maman let me invite you?'

'She won't let you,' I said.

'I don't know about that. Mine and Lélette will be in England, and the twins are too little for your influence to be truly pernicious,' she said, laughing. She grew serious. 'Maman trusts me at the moment. I've had a few tough moments, but I've won her trust; she's no longer afraid that you're going to corrupt me.'

I suspected that Andrée wanted me to come not only because she enjoyed my company but because she wanted to be able to talk to me about Pascal. I didn't mind serving as her confidante, so I was very happy when Andrée told me that I should plan on being free in early September.

★★★

Throughout the month of August, I received only two very short letters from Andrée. She wrote while in bed, at dawn, saying: 'I don't have a minute to myself all day.' She shared a room with her grandmother, who was a light sleeper; any reading or writing she wanted to do had to wait till the light began to filter in through the shutters. The house at Béthary was full of people. There was the fiancé and his two sisters, a pair of languid spinsters who never let Andrée out of their sight, plus a complete set of Rivière de Bonneuil cousins. Even as they celebrated Malou's engagement, Madame Gallard was matchmaking for Andrée; it was a brilliant season, with one party after another. 'This is how I imagine purgatory to be,' Andrée wrote to me. In September she was meant to accompany Malou to her fiancé's parents; the very thought of it was oppressive. Luckily, she received long letters from Pascal.

I couldn't wait to see her again. This year in Sadernac I was very bored; the solitude weighed on me.

Andrée was waiting for me on the platform, in a pink cotton voile dress and a straw cloche. But she wasn't alone: the twins, one in pink gingham, the other in blue, ran up and down the length of the train, calling out 'There's Sylvie! Hello Sylvie!' With their straight hair and dark eyes, they reminded me of the little girl with the burned thigh who had captured my heart ten years earlier, only their cheeks were rounder, and they had a less insolent look in their eyes. Andrée smiled at me, briefly, but with such vivacity that she seemed to me radiant with good health.

'Did you have a good trip?' she asked, holding out her hand.

'When I travel alone, always.'

The little ones looked at us sceptically. 'Why don't you kiss her hello?' the blue twin asked Andrée.

'There are some people you care for quite a lot but don't kiss hello,' said Andrée.

'There are people you kiss hello and don't care for,' said the pink twin.

'Exactly,' said Andrée. 'Carry Sylvie's case to the car,' she added.

The twins grabbed it from me and went skipping off towards the black Citroën parked by the station.

'How are things?' I asked Andrée.

'Neither good nor bad. I'll tell you,' she said. She slipped behind the wheel and I sat next to her; the twins climbed into the back seat, which was filled with parcels. It was clear I had descended on a rigorously organised lifestyle. 'Before you pick up Sylvie, do some errands and come back for the little ones,' Madame Gallard had said. When we got home we would have to unwrap all the parcels. André pulled on her gloves, fiddled with the gears, and as I looked at her more closely, I realised she had grown thin.

'You've lost weight,' I said.

'Maybe a little.'

'Maman yells at her but she doesn't eat anything,' said a twin.

'She doesn't eat anything,' said the other.

'Don't be stupid,' said Andrée. 'If I didn't eat anything, I would be dead.' The car started gently; behind the wheel, in her driving gloves, Andrée looked very competent; though it was true that whatever Andrée did, she did well.

'Do you like to drive?'

'I don't like to play chauffeur all day long,' she answered, 'but I do like to drive.'

The car slid along through the locust trees, but I didn't recognise the road; the steep hill that had made Madame Gallard tighten the bit and the slope the horse had descended with short, tentative steps had all become flat. We arrived quickly. The boxwood had been freshly shaped.

The house hadn't changed, but someone had planted begonias and zinnias by the front steps. 'There weren't flowers here before,' I said.

'No,' said Andrée. 'They're ugly. But now that we have a gardener, he has to have something to do,' she said, her voice turning ironic. She took my bag. 'Tell Maman I'll be right back,' she instructed the twins.

I recognised the hallway and its provincial odour; the stairs squeaked the way I remembered, but on the landing Andrée turned left. 'They've put you in the twins' room; they'll sleep with me and Grand-mère.' She pushed open a door and placed my bag on the ground. 'Maman claims that if we share a room, we won't sleep a wink.'

'That's too bad!' I said.

'It is. But no matter, it's so wonderful that you're here!' said Andrée. 'I'm so happy.'

'Me too.'

'Come down as soon as you're ready. I have to help Maman.'

She closed the door. She wasn't exaggerating when she said she didn't have a minute to herself. Andrée never exaggerated. And yet she had found the time to cut three red roses for me – her favourite flower. I remembered one of her childhood compositions: 'I love roses; they are ceremonial flowers that die without fading, as if with a curtsy.' I opened the armoire to hang up my only dress, a nondescript mauve; I found a robe there, as well as slippers and a pretty white dress with red polka dots. On the dressing table, Andrée had placed a bar of almond soap, a bottle of perfume and rice powder, in a colour that would suit my complexion. It was so thoughtful; I was moved.

Why doesn't she eat? I asked myself. Maybe Madame Gallard had intercepted her letters, but so what? It had been five years since the drama with Bernard – were we going to relive all that? I left my room and went downstairs. It wouldn't be the same as before. Andrée was no longer a child. I felt – I knew – that she loved Pascal incurably. Madame Gallard could find no reason to object to their marriage, I reassured myself; Pascal was so clearly the kind of young man whom you could tell on sight was beyond reproach.

The voices coming from the salon were loud and uproarious; I was intimidated at the thought of going up against all these more or less hostile people. I wasn't a child anymore, either. I went to the library to wait for the dinner bell. I remembered the books, the portraits, the large leather-bound photo album, covered with ornate gilt festoons and astragals, like the mouldings on a ceiling. I undid the metal clasp, and my gaze fell upon a picture of Madame Rivière de Bonneuil. At fifty, she'd worn her hair the same way as she did now, but it was black instead of white; she looked stern, nothing like the sweet old lady she'd become. This woman had made her daughter marry someone against her will. I turned a few pages and examined a picture of

Madame Gallard as a young girl, her neck imprisoned in a guimpe, her hair styled fashionably high above an innocent face in which I recognised Andrée's mouth, severe and generous and unsmiling. There was something attractive in her eyes. I found her again a little further on, sitting next to a bearded gentleman, and smiling at a hideous baby. Something had gone from her eyes. I closed the album and walked to the window, opening it a crack. A breeze flirted in the honesties, sounding their delicate little drums; the swing creaked with no one on it. She was the same age we are, I thought. Under the same stars, she listened to the same night-time rustlings and she swore to herself she wouldn't marry him. Why? He wasn't ugly or stupid; he had many good qualities and a promising future. Did she love someone else? Was there something else she dreamed of doing? And yet today she seemed so utterly to have been born to lead the life she led!

The dinner bell rang and I went to the dining room. I shook many hands, but no one took the time to ask me anything, and I was quickly forgotten. For the entirety of the meal Charles and Henri Rivière de Bonneuil ardently defended *L'Action française* while Monsieur Gallard argued for the Pope.[14] Andrée seemed annoyed. Meanwhile, Madame

[14] In 1926 Pope Pius XI forbid Catholics to read *L'Action française* after it became clear that some of their writers, like Charles Maurras, were agnostic. By 1939 the new pope, Pius XII, lifted the restriction.

Gallard was visibly distracted; I tried, in vain, to find the youthful girl from the album in her yellowed face. And yet she has memories, I said to myself. What are they? And what use does she make of them?

After dinner the men played bridge and the women did arts and crafts. That year, the fashion was for paper hats; you cut thick paper into thin strips that you then moistened to soften them, and then you wove them tightly together and covered the whole thing with a kind of varnish. Andrée was making something green, while the Santenay girls looked on.

'Is it going to be a cloche?' I asked.

'No, a hat with a giant brim,' she said with a knowing smile.

Agnès Santenay asked her to play the violin but Andrée said no. I saw that I wasn't going to be able to talk to her, so I went upstairs and made an early night of it. I didn't spend a single moment with her in the days that followed. In the mornings she was busy around the house; in the afternoons the young people crammed into Charles's and Monsieur Gallard's automobiles to play tennis or go dancing at the neighbouring châteaux, or we descended on some small village for a pelota ball tournament, or to see them race the local cows. Andrée laughed at the appropriate moments. But I still noticed that she ate hardly anything.

One night, I woke to find her pushing open the door to my room.

'Sylvie. Are you asleep?'

She came up to the bed, wrapped in a flannel robe, her feet bare.

'What time is it?'

'One in the morning. If you're not too tired let's go downstairs – it'll be better to talk down there, up here they can hear us.'

I slipped on my dressing gown and we went quietly down the stairs, avoiding the ones that creaked. Andrée went into the library and lit a lamp.

'The other nights, I couldn't get out of bed without waking up Grand-mère. It's amazing how lightly old people sleep.'

'I've so wanted to talk with you,' I said.

'Me too, of course!' Andrée sighed. 'It's been like this since the beginning of the summer. Bad luck. This year more than others I've just wanted to be left in peace!'

'Your mother still doesn't suspect anything?' I asked.

'If only!' Andrée said. 'She finally noticed all these envelopes addressed to me in a man's handwriting. Last week she grilled me about them.' Andrée shrugged. 'I was going to have to tell her about him sooner or later.'

'So? What did she say?'

'I told her everything,' said Andrée. 'She didn't ask to read Pascal's letters, and I wouldn't have shown them to her, but I told her the whole story. She didn't forbid me to carry on writing to him. She said she needs to think about it.' Andrée scanned the room, as if she were looking around for help. The dour books and ancestors were not very reassuring.

'Did she seem upset? When will you know her decision?'

'I have no idea,' said Andrée. 'She didn't really say anything, she just asked me questions. She was so curt with me. "I need to think about it."'

'There's no reason for her to take against Pascal,' I said warmly. 'Even from her perspective, he's not a bad match.'

'I don't know. In our circle, marriages aren't made like that.' She added bitterly, 'Everyone's suspicious if you marry for love.'

'But they can't keep you from marrying Pascal merely because you love him!'

'I don't know,' Andrée said, distracted. She shot a glance at me then looked away. 'I don't even know if Pascal is thinking of marrying me.'

'He's never talked about it because it's obvious!' I said. 'For Pascal, loving you and wanting to marry you is the same thing.'

'He's never said that he loves me,' she said.

'I know. But in Paris, the last few months, you felt very sure that he did. And you were right. Anyone could see it.'

Andrée toyed with her necklace; she didn't speak for a moment.

'In my first letter, I told Pascal that I loved him. Maybe that was wrong, but I don't know how to explain it to you: in a letter, keeping it to myself seemed like a lie.'

I nodded. Andrée had always been incapable of lying.

'He replied with a very beautiful letter,' said Andrée. 'But he said that he didn't feel he had the right to say the word *love*. He explained that in his secular life as in his religious one, nothing was self-evident; he needed to verify his feelings through experience.'

'Don't worry about that,' I said. 'Pascal has always criticised me for deciding my opinions instead of putting them to the test – that's just how he is! He needs to take his time. But his experience will quickly bear out his feelings.'

I knew Pascal well enough to be sure that he wasn't playing a game; but I loathed his reticence. Andrée would have been sleeping and eating better if she were more confident of his love.

'Did you tell him that you spoke with your mother?'

'Yes.'

'You'll see. As soon as he's worried that your relationship is at risk, he'll have the validation he needs.'

Andrée fiddled with her necklace, biting one of the medallions. 'I guess I'll just have to wait,' she said without conviction.

'Honestly, Andrée, can you imagine Pascal in love with another woman?'

She hesitated. 'He might discover that marriage isn't his calling.'

'You don't think he still wants to be a priest!'

'He might still be thinking about it if he hadn't met me,' said Andrée. 'Maybe I'm a trap that was placed in his way to make him deviate from his true path ...'

I couldn't believe what I was hearing. Pascal had called her a Jansenist, but it was worse than that: she suspected God of diabolical machinations. 'That's absurd,' I said. 'If pushed to it I can imagine God tempting people, but not misleading them.'

Andrée shrugged. 'They say that you should have faith precisely because the idea of it is absurd. So I end up thinking that the more absurd things seem, the greater the chance they have of being true.'

We talked for a few more minutes, but suddenly the library door opened. 'What are you doing in there?' asked a little voice. It was Dédé, the pink twin, Andrée's favourite of the two.

'I could ask the same of you,' said Andrée. 'Why aren't you in bed?'

Dédé came closer to us, lifting up her long white nightshirt in her hands. 'Grand-mère woke me up by turning on the light. She asked where you were. I said I would go and see ...'

Andrée got up. 'Be a lamb. I'm going to tell Grand-mère that I couldn't sleep and that I came down to the library to read. Don't tell her about Sylvie; Maman will be cross with me.'

'That's telling a lie,' said Dédé.

'I'll be the one telling a lie, you just have to keep quiet, that's not lying.' Andrée added, convincingly, 'When you grow up, it's sometimes alright to lie.'

'It sounds nice to be grown up,' Dédé said with a sigh.

'There's good and there's bad,' Andrée said, stroking her head.

I went back up to my room. She's their slave, I thought. Not a single move she makes isn't regulated by the mother or the grandmother, and immediately made to serve as a lesson for the little ones. Not a single thought in her head isn't answerable to God!

That's the worst part, I thought the next day, while Andrée prayed beside me in the pew that a copper plate identified as having belonged to the Rivière de Bonneuil family for nearly a century. Madame Gallard played the harmonium, the twins marched down the aisle holding baskets full of the blessèd brioche, and Andrée spoke to God with her head in her hands. With what words? She must not have an easy relationship with Him. I was sure of one thing: she could not manage to convince herself that He was good, and yet she didn't want to displease Him, and she tried to love Him. Things would have been simpler if, like me, she had lost her faith when her faith lost its naïveté. I watched the twins. They were busy and important; at their age, religion is an amusing game. I had brandished oriflammes and scattered rose petals before the gilt-encrusted priests carrying the sacred sacrament; I had paraded around in a communion dress and kissed the enormous violet stones in the bishops' rings – the altar of repose, the May altars to the Virgin Mary, the nativity scenes, the processions, the angels, the incense, all those scents, the choreography, all the extravagant trappings had been the only luxury of my childhood. It felt so right, being dazzled by all that magnificence, feeling your soul float above your head, white and shining like the Host at the heart of the monstrance! And then, one day, soul and heaven darken, and you find that remorse, sin and fear have taken up residence. Even when she restricted herself to thinking about earthly things, Andrée took everything happening around her terribly to heart. How could she not have been seized by anguish to envision her life in the mysterious light of the supernatural world? To stand up to her mother would be like revolting against God Himself. But perhaps in being submissive, she showed herself unworthy of the graces she had received. How was she to know whether in loving Pascal she were not carrying out Satan's designs? Every moment, all of eternity was at stake, and there was no clear indication whether she was about to win or lose! Pascal had helped Andrée to overcome these fears. But our night-time conversation showed me that she had quickly fallen prey to them again. It was certainly not in church that her heart found peace.

I felt the stress of it all afternoon, and I took no pleasure in watching cows with sharpened horns charged by young fear-stricken country boys. For the next three days, all the women in the house laboured away in the basement; I shelled peas and pitted prunes. Every year, the great landowners in the region got together on the banks of the Adour and ate cold food; this seemingly casual party required extensive preparations. 'Each family has to outdo the others, and every year has to be better than the one before,' said Andrée. When the morning arrived, we filled a hired van with two large hampers full of food and dishes, and the young men and women squeezed themselves into whatever space remained. The older people and the fiancés drove behind. I wore the polka-dotted dress Andrée had lent me; she wore one of raw silk with a green belt that matched her wide-brimmed hat, which you almost couldn't tell was made of paper.

The water was blue, the oak trees ancient, the grass thick; we would have sat in it nibbling on sandwiches and talking until evening, and it would have been a perfectly blissful afternoon, I thought sadly as I helped Andrée unwrap the hampers and baskets. What a to-do! The tables had to be set up, the buffet spread, the tablecloths laid out in the right places. Other cars arrived, some shiny and new, others antique, even a break pulled by two horses.

The young people immediately started laying out dishes. The older people sat against tarpaulin-wrapped tree trunks, or on folding chairs. Andrée smiled and curtsied at them; the older men particularly liked her, and she had long talks with them. In between conversations, she relieved Malou and Guite, who were turning the crank on a complicated machine that turned cream into ice cream. I helped them as well.

'Would you look at that!' I said, looking at the tables covered in food.

'Yes, when it comes to fulfilling our social duties we are first-rate Christians!' said Andrée.

The cream wouldn't harden. We gave up, and arranged ourselves on one of the tablecloths, along with the other young people. Cousin Charles was speaking in a distinguished voice with a young girl who was very ugly but marvellously dressed; we didn't even have the words for the colour or the fabric of her dress.

'It's like a debutante ball, this picnic,' said Andrée.[15]

'Is she being presented to him? She's very unattractive,' I said.

[15] She actually says it's like 'le bal des liserés verts', a gala given by the Club National des Liserés Verts, founded in September 1922 with the philanthropic aim of organising marriages through taking young people on outings and trips.

'But very rich,' said Andrée, with a little laugh. 'There are at least ten different men in the running.'

In those days, I had a voracious appetite, but the abundance and the solemnity of the trays the servants were passing around put me off. Fish in aspic, stuffed sliced ham, barquettes, galantines, ballotines, daubes, chauds-froids, pâtés, terrines, confits, dodines, mixed diced vegetables with mayonnaise, pies, frangipane tarts – you were expected to taste a little of everything so as to offend no one. Andrée ate more than usual, and when the meal began she was almost cheerful. Her neighbour on her right, a smug handsome man with dark hair, kept trying to meet her gaze, and spoke to her in a low voice. She soon seemed irritated, and anger or wine put colour in her cheeks. All the neighbouring winemakers had brought bottles; we drank most of them. The conversation grew more animated. We started talking about flirting. Was it permissible to flirt? Up to what point? In the end everyone was against it, but it provided for many giddy private conversations between the girls and boys. Overall, these young people were strait-laced, but some were pretty vulgar; there was quite a lot of naughty giggling, and these titillated young people began telling stories that sounded officially above board, but in a way that suggested they could well tell others. We opened a magnum of champagne, and someone said we should all drink from the same glass so each could learn the thoughts of the person next to them. The coupe was passed from hand to hand; when the smug handsome brown-haired man emptied it, he whispered something in Andrée's ear while he handed her the glass. With a wave of her hand she knocked it onto the grass. 'I prefer to keep my thoughts to myself,' she said curtly.

There was an embarrassed silence. Charles burst out laughing. 'Little Andrée doesn't want us to find out her secrets?'

'I don't pry into anyone else's,' she said. 'And in any case I've already had enough to drink.' She stood up. 'I'm going to find some coffee.'

I watched her, perplexed. I would have sipped the champagne without objection. Yes, there was something unsettling in this innocent libertinage, but what did that concern us? Doubtless it struck Andrée as a sacrilege, these two mouths supposedly meeting by sharing a glass; was she thinking of Bernard's long-ago kisses, or those she had yet to receive from Pascal? Andrée didn't come back, so I stood up and took refuge in the shade of the oak trees. Again I wondered what she had meant by 'non-platonic' kisses. I was well informed when it came to sexual problems; during childhood and adolescence my body had dreamed its dreams; but neither my considerable studies nor my negligible experience explained what connected the body's metamorphoses to tenderness, and happiness.

For Andrée, there was a passageway between the heart and the body that remained a mystery to me.

I emerged from the copse. The river curved, and I found myself on its banks. I heard the noise of a waterfall; beneath the clear water the gemstone-like pebbles looked like boiled sweets pretending to be pebbles.

'Sylvie!' It was Madame Gallard, red-faced beneath her straw hat. 'Do you know where Andrée is?'

'I'm looking for her,' I said.

'She's been gone an hour, it's very rude.'

She really is worried, I thought. No doubt she loved Andrée in her way, but what way was that? That was the question. We all loved her, only differently.

The waterfall crashed noisily in our ears. Madame Gallard stopped short.

'I knew it!'

Under a tree, near a tuft of autumn crocuses, I saw Andrée's dress, her green belt, her coarse linen undergarments. Madame Gallard went to the river. 'Andrée!'

Something moved at the foot of the waterfall. Andrée's head appeared.

'Come on in! The water's amazing!'

'Will you come out of there at once!'

Andrée swam towards us, laugher on her face.

'And so soon after eating! You'll have a stomach ache!' said Madame Gallard.

Andrée rose up from the riverbank; she was wrapped in a loden cape that she had fastened with hairpins. Her hair hung straight down over her eyes.

'Ah! You look very healthy,' said Madame Gallard, her voice softening. 'How are you going to dry yourself off?'

'I'll figure something out.'

'What was the Good Lord thinking when he gave me such a daughter!' said Madame Gallard; she was smiling, but she added, more severely, 'Come back right away. You're neglecting your duties.'

'I'm coming.'

Madame Gallard went off and I sat on the other side of a tree while Andrée got dressed.

'It was so nice in the water!'

'It must have been freezing.'

'When the waterfall hit my back, it knocked the wind out of me,' said Andrée, 'but it felt good.'

I picked a crocus, and wondered if they really were poisonous, these funny flowers which in their plainness managed to be both rustic and sophisticated, and which came out of the ground in a single burst, like mushrooms.

'Do you think that if we made a broth for the Santenay sisters from autumn crocuses they would die from it?' I asked.

'Poor things! They mean well, you know,' Andrée said. She came close to me. She had put her dress back on, and she was tying her belt. 'I dried myself off with my petticoat.

No one will see that I'm not wearing it anymore; we always have too many clothes on anyway.' She spread out her wet cape and the wrinkled skirt. 'We have to go back.'

'Alas!'

'Poor Sylvie! You must be very bored.' She smiled at me. 'Now that the picnic is over, I hope I'll have more free time.'

'Do you think you could arrange it so we can see each other a bit?'

'One way or another, I'll arrange it.' As we walked slowly along the riverbank, she told me she'd had a letter from Pascal that morning.

'A good one?'

She nodded. 'Yes.' She rubbed a mint leaf between her fingers and breathed it in. She seemed happy. 'He said that if Maman has asked to think it over, that's a good sign. He said I should be more confident.'

'That's what I think too.'

'I'm confident,' said Andrée.

I wanted to ask her why she'd thrown the champagne coupe on the ground, but I was afraid of troubling her.

Andrée charmed everyone for the rest of the day; I didn't really enjoy myself. And in the days that followed, she had no more freedom than she'd had. There was no doubt. Madame Gallard had purposefully arranged things to prevent us from seeing each other. When she had discovered Pascal's letters, she must have regretted having invited me, and she was trying to control the damage as best she could. I grew wistful as the time approached for me to leave. When they returned to Paris, Malou would be married, and Andrée would replace her sister at home and in the world; I would only be able to see her in rushed moments between a charity bazaar and a funeral. A couple of days before I left, as I had grown accustomed to doing, I went for a walk on the grounds while everyone was still sleeping. The summer was ending, the hedges were reddening, the red berries on the rowan tree were turning yellow; in the white light of morning, the autumn leaves seemed even more insistent. I liked the contrast between the flaming red trees and the grass still smoking from the frost. Filled with melancholy, I walked along the well-raked paths where the flowers no longer grew, and I thought I heard a violin. At the very end of the park, hidden by a cluster of pine trees, Andrée was playing. She had thrown an old shawl around her blue jersey dress, and she seemed to be listening prayerfully to the voice of the instrument on her shoulder. Her beautiful black hair was parted obediently on one side; the line of her scalp was a touching shade of white that made you want to run your finger along it with tenderness and respect. For a moment I watched Andrée as she moved the bow back and forth over the strings, and thought how alone she looked.

The last note died out, and I went up to her, breaking pine needles under my feet. 'Oh!' said Andrée. 'You heard me? Can you hear me from the house?'

'No,' I said. 'I was out walking this way. You play so well!'

Andrée sighed. 'If only I had more time to practise.'

'Do you often give these outdoor concerts?'

'No. But for the last few days I've wanted to play so badly! and I didn't want any of those people to hear me.' Andrée placed the violin in its little coffin. 'I have to go back before Maman comes down; she'll say that I'm crazy and that won't help matters.'

'Will you bring your violin with you to the Santenays'?' I asked, as we walked back to the house.

'Of course not! Oh, this trip. The very thought of it is appalling. At least here I feel at home.'

'Do you really have to go?'

'I don't want to fight Maman over things that don't matter. Especially not now.'

'I understand,' I said.

Andrée went back into the house, and I settled myself down in the grass with a book. A bit later, I saw her cutting roses with the Santenay sisters. And then she went to chop some wood in the shed; I heard the dull blows of the axe. The sun rose in the sky and I read joylessly. I no longer felt at all sure that Madame Gallard's decision would be a positive one. Like her sister, Andrée had only a modest dowry, but she was much prettier and brighter than Malou, and her mother no doubt harboured greater ambitions for her.

Suddenly someone cried out. The voice was Andrée's.

I ran to the woodshed. Madame Gallard was leaning over her; Andrée was lying in the sawdust, eyes closed, bleeding from her foot; the edge of the axe was stained red.

'Malou, get your first-aid kit, Andrée's hurt!' Madame Gallard shouted. She asked me to go and ring for the doctor. When I came back, Malou was wrapping Andrée's foot and her mother was giving her ammonia to inhale. She opened her eyes. 'The axe got away from me!'

'It didn't touch the bone,' said Malou. 'It's a deep cut, but it didn't touch the bone.'

Andrée had a light fever, and the doctor thought she was exhausted; he prescribed a lot of rest. In any case, she wouldn't be able to walk on her foot for a couple of weeks.

When I went to see her that evening, she was very pale but she gave me a big smile. 'I'm stuck in bed until the end of the summer!' she said in a triumphant voice.

'Does it hurt?'

'Hardly!' she said. 'But even if it were ten times worse, it would be better than going to the Santenays',' she added. She looked impish. 'That is what they call a providential accident.'

'Andrée!' I stared at her in puzzlement. 'You don't mean to say you did it on purpose?'

'I could never think to bother Providence over something so small,' she said happily.

'How could you bring yourself to do it! You could have cut your foot off!'

Andrée lay back and turned her head against the pillow. 'I couldn't take it anymore,' she said.

For a moment she looked up at the ceiling without speaking, and looking at her ashen face, her staring eyes, I felt an old fear reassert itself. To pick up the axe, and to strike – I would not have been capable. My blood rebelled at the very thought of it. Whatever she had been thinking at precisely the moment she did it terrified me.

'Does your mother suspect anything?'

'I don't think so.' Andrée sat up. 'I told you I would figure out a way to free up some time, one way or another.'

'Did you know what you were going to do?'

'I knew I was going to do something. The idea of the axe occurred to me this morning as I was picking flowers. First I thought of hurting myself with the pruners but it wouldn't have been enough.'

'You scare me,' I said.

Andrée gave me a wide smile. 'Why? I did it right, I didn't use too much force. Do you want me to see if Maman will let you stay till the end of the month?'

'She won't let me.'

'Let me speak to her!'

Did Madame Gallard suspect the truth? Did it make her remorseful, or fearful? Or was it the doctor's diagnosis that worried her? Either way, she agreed that I could stay at Béthary to keep Andrée company. The Rivière de Bonneuils left at the same time as Malou and the Santenays, and from one day to the next the house went quiet. Andrée had a room to herself, and I spent long hours at her side. One morning, she told me she'd had a long conversation with her mother about Pascal the night before.

'And?'

Andrée lit a cigarette; she smoked when she was nervous. 'She talked it over with Papa. They have nothing in particular against Pascal; he even made a good impression on them when you brought him to the house with you that time.' She sought my gaze. 'But I understand Maman. She doesn't know Pascal; she wonders if his intentions are serious.'

'She's not against the idea of marrying him?' I asked, hopeful.

'No.'

'Well that's the important thing!' I said. 'Aren't you happy?'

Andrée took a drag. 'They won't entertain the idea of marriage for at least two or three years.'

'I know.'

'Maman wants us to be officially engaged. Otherwise I'm not allowed to see Pascal. She wants to send me to England, to cut us off from each other.'

'You'll just have to get engaged, that's all.' I went on, in a bright voice, 'I know you haven't raised the question with Pascal, but you can't imagine he'll let you go for two years!'

'I can't force him to be my fiancé!' Andrée said, agitated. 'He asked me to be patient, he said he needs time to see within himself more clearly; I can't throw myself at his feet saying "Marry me!"'

'You wouldn't throw yourself at his feet; you would explain the situation.'

'It would be the same thing, I'd be cornering him.'

'It's not your fault! You have no other choice.'

She struggled with the idea for a while, but I finally convinced her to speak to Pascal. Only she refused to tell him the situation by letter; she told her mother that she would speak to him when they returned to Paris. Madame Gallard agreed. She smiled a lot, in those days; maybe she was proud of having two daughters settled. She was almost friendly with me; and often, when she fixed Andrée's pillows, or slipped a bedjacket around her shoulders, I saw something in her eyes that reminded me of the young girl in the photograph.

Andrée had written to Pascal describing playfully what happened, how she'd got hurt, and received two concerned letters in response. He said that she needed someone reasonable to watch over her, and other things as well that she didn't tell me about, but I understood that she no longer was in any doubt about his feelings for her. Resting, and getting more sleep, put some colour back in her cheeks and she even gained a little weight. I had never seen her so thriving as the day she could finally get out of bed.

She limped a little; it was hard for her to walk. Monsieur Gallard lent us his Citroën for a whole day. I had only been in an automobile a few times, and never just for the pleasure of it. My heart was overjoyed as I took my place beside Andrée and the car slid along the avenue, with all the windows down. We drove through the forest, following a long, straight road that stretched out in front of us, getting lost among the pine trees disappearing into the sky. Andrée drove very quickly – the speedometer reached 80 km/h! Though she was a competent driver, I was a little worried.

'You're not going to try to kill us?' I asked.

'Of course not!' She smiled happily. 'I don't want to die anymore.'

'But before you wanted to?'

'Oh, yes! Every night when I went to sleep I prayed not to wake up. Now I pray to God to keep me alive,' she added gaily.

We left the main road and slowly skirted the still ponds among the heather; we had lunch by the sea, in a deserted hotel. The season was over; the beaches were abandoned, the villas shuttered. At Bayonne, we bought multicoloured bars of nougat for the twins; we ate one while we slowly walked around the cloister of the cathedral. Andrée leaned on my shoulder. We talked about the cloisters in Spain and Italy where we would walk one day, and other, farther-off countries, the trips we would take. As we returned to the car, I gestured at her bandaged foot. 'I will never understand how you had the courage to do that.'

'You would have, if you'd felt trapped like I did.' She touched her temple. 'I was having the most terrible headaches.'

'You don't have them anymore?'

'Much less frequently. Since I wasn't sleeping at night, I was taking far too much maxiton and kola.'[16]

'You're not going to start that again?'

'No. When we get back, it will be painful for a couple of weeks, until Malou's wedding; but now I feel more up to it.'

We drove back to the forest along a little road that took us past the Adour. Madame Gallard had still managed to think of an errand for Andrée: she had to drop off a layette Madame Rivière de Bonneuil had knitted for a local woman who was expecting a baby. Andrée stopped the car in front of a pretty Landaise house, in the middle

[16] An amphetamine and a source of caffeine (kola nuts).

of a clearing surrounded by pine trees. I was used to the tenant farms of Sadernac, to the heaps of manure and the puddles of liquid dung, and was surprised by the elegance of this farm lost in the forest. The young woman offered us some rosé wine that her father-in-law had made himself; she opened her armoire so we could admire her embroidered sheets, and the odour of lavender and sweet clover drifted out. A ten-month-old baby laughed in his Moses basket, and Andrée shook her necklace to amuse him; she had always loved babies. 'He's so alert for his age!' Andrée said. Coming from her, conversational niceties shed their banality, so sincere was her voice, her smile.

'That one never sleeps, either,' his mother said, smiling, placing a hand on his belly. She was dark-haired, with an olive complexion, like Andrée; she had the same build, though her legs were perhaps a bit shorter, and had a graceful way about her in spite of her advanced pregnancy. When Andrée is pregnant, she'll be just like that, I thought. For the first time I was able to picture Andrée married with children, without worrying. She would be surrounded by lustrous, well-made furniture, like there was in the house; you would feel at ease in her home. But she wouldn't spend hours polishing the silver or covering pots of jam with parchment paper; she would play her violin and – I was secretly convinced – she would write books. She had always loved books, and writing. Happiness suits her so well, I thought, as she spoke with the young mother about her babies, the one she was expecting and the one who was beginning to cut his teeth.

'What a beautiful day!' I said, an hour later, when the car pulled up in front of the flower beds.

Andrée agreed. I was sure that she, too, had thought about the future.

★★★

The Gallards headed back to Paris before me, because of Malou's wedding. As soon as I got back, I telephoned Andrée and we agreed to meet the following day; she seemed in a hurry to hang up, and I wanted to see her face while we spoke. I didn't ask her any questions.

I waited for her in the gardens of the Champs-Élysées, facing the statue of Alphonse Daudet. She arrived slightly late, and I saw right away that something was wrong. She sat beside me and didn't even try to smile at me.

'Is everything alright?'

'No,' she said, and added, in a dull voice, 'Pascal doesn't want to.'

'Doesn't want to what?'

'Doesn't want to get engaged. Not now.'

'So?'

'So Maman is sending me to Cambridge right after the wedding.'

'But that's absurd!' I said. 'Impossible. Pascal can't let you go like that.'

'He said that we would write to each other, that he would try to visit at least once, that two years isn't very long,' said Andrée in her oddly inexpressive voice. She sounded like she was reciting a catechism in which she'd long since lost faith.

'But why?' I asked.

Usually, when Andrée recounted a conversation, it was with such clarity that it seemed like I could hear it with my own ears, but this time, I couldn't make much sense of it. Pascal had seemed emotional when he saw her again, he told her that he loved her, but when she mentioned the word *engagement*, his face had changed. No, he'd said vigorously, no! His father would never let him marry so young; after all the sacrifices he had made for Pascal, Monsieur Blondel had the right to expect his son to dedicate himself, body and soul, to passing the *agrégation*. A love affair would look like a distraction from his studies. I knew that Pascal greatly respected his father, and I could understand that his first instinct was to worry about hurting him, but when he knew that Madame Gallard wouldn't budge, how could he not risk being slightly disobedient?

'Did he see how much the idea of this trip made you unhappy?'

'I don't know.'

'Did you tell him?'

'A little.'

'You have to make him understand. I'm sure you didn't try hard enough to make him see.'

'He seemed trapped,' said Andrée. 'I know what that feels like!' Her voice trembled, and I saw that she hadn't dared venture further into the matter with Pascal, that she hadn't tried to refute his arguments.

'There's still time to fight this.'

'Must I spend my life fighting against the people I love?' She spoke with such violence that I didn't continue. I thought it over.

'What if Pascal explained his situation to your mother?'

'I suggested it to her. It isn't enough. She says that if Pascal had serious intentions of marrying me, he would have introduced me to his family. Because he won't, the only thing to do is to cut it off. Maman has a funny way of putting it,' said Andrée. She looked thoughtful. 'She said: "I know you so well, you are my daughter, you are my own flesh and blood, you aren't strong enough to be left at the mercy of temptation; if you gave in, I would deserve to have the sin fall equally upon my own head."'

Her gaze was questioning, as if she were hoping that I could help her unearth the hidden meaning behind these words, but for the moment, I was helplessly perplexed by the private dramas of Madame Gallard. The way Andrée had resigned herself to the situation exasperated me. 'What if you refused to go?' I asked.

'Refuse? How?'

'They can't force you to get on a boat.'

'I could shut myself up in my room, go on a hunger strike,' said Andrée, 'but what then? Maman would go and speak with Pascal's father ...' She hid her face in her hands. 'I don't want to think of Maman as the enemy! It's awful!'

'I will speak to Pascal,' I said with decisiveness. 'You didn't go about it the right way.'

'You won't get anywhere.'

'Let me try.'

'Try, but you won't get anywhere.' Andrée gave the statue of Alphonse Daudet a hard look, but her eyes focused on something beside the languid marble. 'God is against me,' she said.

I shivered at the blasphemy, as if I were still a believer. 'Pascal would say you were a blasphemer,' I said. 'If God exists, He isn't against anyone.'

'What do either of you know? Who can understand what God is?' she said. She shrugged. 'Oh, well, maybe He's saving me a comfortable place in heaven, but on this earth, He is against me.'

And yet, she added in an impassioned voice, there were people in heaven who were happy in this world! She burst into tears. 'I don't want to go! Two years far from Pascal, from Maman, from you – I wouldn't survive it!'

Never, not even when she had broken things off with Bernard, had I ever seen Andrée cry. I wanted to take her hand, make some gesture, but I was imprisoned by our strict upbringing, and I didn't move. I thought of the hours she had spent on the roof of the château de Béthary asking herself if she was going to jump; in this particular moment, everything inside of her was just as dark.

'Andrée,' I said. 'You won't have to go. I'm certain I'll be able to convince Pascal.'

She wiped her eyes, looked at her watch and stood up.

'You won't get anywhere.'

I was sure she was wrong. When I telephoned Pascal that evening, his voice was light and gay; he loved Andrée, and he could be reasoned with. Andrée had failed because she had gone in expecting to; I would win him over and carry the day.

Pascal was waiting for me on the terrace of the Luxembourg; he always arrived early to meetings. I sat down, and we said something about how beautiful the day was. The surface of the pond was criss-crossed with miniature sailing boats, and the flower beds looked as though they'd been embroidered; between their orderly design and the clear skies, I was convinced what I was about to say was good sense – truthful, good sense. I launched my assault.

'I saw Andrée yesterday afternoon.'

Pascal looked at me, comprehending. 'I also wanted to discuss Andrée with you. Sylvie, you have to help me.'

These were the exact words Madame Gallard had once used with me. 'No! I won't help you persuade Andrée to go to England. She cannot go! She may not have told you how much the idea terrifies her, but I know.'

'She told me, and that's why I need you to help me. She has to understand that being apart for two years isn't a tragedy.'

'It would be for her,' I said. 'It's not only you she'd be leaving, but her entire life. I've never seen her this miserable,' I added with vehemence. 'You can't inflict this on her!'

'You know Andrée,' said Pascal. 'You know she always starts out by taking things too much to heart, but her feelings eventually balance out.' He went on: 'If Andrée leaves of her own accord, sure of my love for her, confident of our future, it won't be so terrible to be apart!'

'How can you expect her to be sure of your love for her, and confident, and so on, if you let her go like this!' I said. I looked at him with consternation. 'It is entirely up to you whether she is completely happy or completely miserable. And yet you choose to make her miserable.'

'You have a talent for simplifying things,' said Pascal. He caught a hoop which a little girl had just hurled at his legs, and sent it back to her with a precise gesture. 'Being happy, or being miserable, is entirely a question of outlook.'

'In her present outlook, Andrée will cry all day long,' I said. I added, irritated, 'She isn't as reasoned in her feelings as you are! When she loves someone, she wants to be near them.'

'Why should being in love be an excuse for being unreasonable?' said Pascal. 'I hate these romantic preconceptions.' He shrugged. 'Presence, in the physical sense of the term, isn't that important. Or otherwise it takes on too much importance.'

'Maybe Andrée is romantic, maybe she's wrong, but if you love her, you should try to understand her. Reasoning won't change her mind.' I cast a worried look at the flower beds of heliotrope and salvia, and thought to myself: reasoning won't change Pascal's mind.

'Why are you so afraid to speak to your father about it?' I asked.

'It's not that I'm afraid,' said Pascal.

'What is it then?'

'I explained it to Andrée.'

'She didn't understand.'

'You have to know my father, and the relationship I have with him.' He looked at me reproachfully. 'Sylvie, you know that I know Andrée, don't you?'

'I know that you are driving her to desperation in order to spare your father the least bit of worry. Come on!' I said, impatiently, 'surely he knows you're going to get married one day!'

'He would think it was absurd to marry so young. He would judge Andrée too harshly, and he would lose all respect for me.' Again he sought my gaze. 'I love Andrée. You have to believe that my reasons are serious, to refuse what she's asking of me.'

'I don't understand them.'

Pascal thought for a moment, and made a gesture of powerlessness. 'My father is old, and tired. It's so sad to get old!' he said in an emotional voice.

'You could at least try to explain the situation to him. Make him see that Andrée can't bear this separation.'

'He will tell me that we can bear anything,' said Pascal. 'You know, he himself has been through quite a lot. I am sure he will think this separation is desirable.'

'But why?' I asked. I was detecting an obstinance in Pascal that frightened me. And yet there was only one sky above our heads, only one truth.

An idea came to me in a flash. 'Have you spoken to your sister about it?'

'My sister? No. Why?'

'Talk to her. Maybe she can think of a way to present things to your father.'

Pascal was quiet for a moment. 'My sister would be even more upset than he would be, if I got engaged.'

I thought of Emma, her large forehead, her navy-blue dress with its lace piqué collar, and the air of ownership she had when she spoke of Pascal. Of course. She was not on our side.

'Ah,' I said. 'It's Emma you're afraid of.'

'Why do you refuse to understand?' said Pascal. 'I will not cause pain to either my father or to Emma, after everything they've done for me. That seems completely normal to me.'

'Emma isn't still hoping you're going to enter the seminary?'

'Of course not.' He hesitated. 'It's no fun to get old, and it's no fun to live with an old person. When I move out, the house will be so sad for my sister.'

Yes, I understood Emma's perspective, much more than Monsieur Blondel's. I wondered if it wasn't actually because of her that Pascal was so intent on keeping his affections a secret.

'They must resign themselves to seeing you leave, one day!' I said.

'I'm only asking for Andrée to be patient for two years,' said Pascal. 'And at that point, my father will think it's normal for me to get married, and Emma will have had time to get used to the idea. Today, it would tear them to pieces.'

'Having to go to England will tear Andrée to pieces. If someone has to suffer, why should it be her?'

'Andrée and I have our lives ahead of us, and the knowledge that later on, we will be happy. We can well manage to sacrifice ourselves for a moment for those who have nothing to look forward to,' said Pascal with a note of irritation.

'She will suffer more than you,' I said. I looked at Pascal with hostility. 'She is young, yes, that means she has blood running through her veins, she wants to live …'

Pascal nodded. 'That's another reason why this separation is a good idea,' he said.

I was taken aback. 'What do you mean?'

'Sylvie, in some ways you are quite undeveloped for your age,' he told me, in the same tone which Abbé Dominique had once used to lecture me during my confessions. 'Besides which, there are certain matters which escape you, because you have lost your faith.'

'For example?'

'The kind of intimacy that arises between two people who are engaged to be married greatly tests a Christian's resolve. Andrée is a real, flesh and blood woman. Even if we didn't indulge our desires, they would still be with us, inescapably. This kind of fixation is in itself a sin.'

I felt myself go red. I hadn't anticipated this argument, and I didn't like thinking about it. 'If Andrée is ready to take that risk, it's not up to you to decide for her,' I said.

'But it is, it's my job to protect her from herself. Andrée is so generous that she would damn herself for love.'

'Poor Andrée! All anyone wants is to protect her. And all she wants is a little happiness on this earth!'

'Andrée has more of a developed sense of sin than I do,' he said. 'I've seen her blush with regret over an innocent childhood infatuation. If our own relations became more entangled, she would never forgive herself.'

I sensed that I was losing the argument, and my anxiety strengthened my resolve. 'Pascal,' I said, 'listen to me. I have just spent a month with Andrée. She can't take much more of this. Physically she's somewhat recovered, but she will lose her appetite again and stop sleeping, and she'll wind up getting sick. She is at her wits' end. Imagine the state of mind she must have been in, to stick an axe in her foot?' Barely pausing for breath, I described what Andrée's life had been for the previous five years. How she'd been torn away from Bernard, and disillusioned by the truth of the world she lived in, how she'd fought against her mother for the right to follow her heart and her conscience; all her victories were poisoned by remorse, and in the least of her desires she suspected a sin. As I spoke, I realised the deep, irreconcilable divisions that lay within Andrée, which she had never revealed to me but which I sensed from some of the things she'd said. I began to be afraid, and it seemed to me that Pascal should be as well.

'Every night for five years she wished to die,' I said. 'And the other day she sounded so hopeless. She said to me: "God is against me!"'

Pascal shook his head; his face hadn't changed. 'I know Andrée as well as you,' he said, 'and even better, because

I can follow her down paths from which you are excluded. He has made many demands of her. But what you are not aware of is that God dispenses grace in the same degree as He inflicts struggle. Andrée has joys and consolations that you don't know anything about.'

I couldn't argue with him any longer. I got up and left, and went walking with my head down under the lying sky. Other arguments came to mind, but they would have been useless. It was strange. We had had hundreds of conversations, and today was the first time neither of us had conquered the other. Today, something very real was at stake, and all our reasonings broke against the beliefs that stubbornly dwelled within us. In the following days I often asked myself where Pascal's real obedience lay. Was it his father or Emma who intimidated him? Did he believe these stories of temptation and sin? Or was that all just an excuse? Was he himself unwilling to engage himself in his future life as an adult? He had always viewed the future with such apprehension. If only Madame Gallard had not insisted on this engagement; Pascal could have calmly visited Andrée during these two years; the depth of their love would have persuaded him, he would have got used to the idea of becoming a man. His stubbornness was galling. I was angry at Madame Gallard, at Pascal, and not least at myself, because too many things about Andrée remained incomprehensible to me, and so I could not help her.

Three days passed before Andrée could find time to see me again. She told me to meet her at the tea room at Printemps, where all around me perfumed women ate cake and talked about the cost of living. From the day she was born, Andrée was fated to be like them. But she was nothing like them. I tried to find the words to tell her what I had to say; I couldn't find any to console even myself.

Andrée came bounding in. 'I'm late!'

'It doesn't matter.' She was often late, not because she didn't care, but because she had too many contradictory cares.

'I'm so sorry to have asked you to meet me here, but I'm so pressed for time,' she said. She put her purse on the table, along with a collection of fabric samples. 'I've already been to four shops!'

'What a life!' I said. I knew the routine. When the little Gallards needed a coat or a dress, Andrée went round to the department stores and a few specialised boutiques, gathering samples to take home, where, after a family consultation, Madame Gallard would choose one, taking into account its quality and price. This time, they needed things to wear for the wedding; such matters could not be resolved lightly.

'Your parents are not exactly hurting for a hundred francs,' I said with impatience.

'No, but they still don't like to waste money,' she said.

It wouldn't have been a waste, I thought, to spare Andrée the fatigue and boredom of such complicated errands. There were circles under her eyes, and her make-up was smeared across her pale skin. Still, to my great surprise, she smiled. 'I think the twins will be adorable in this blue silk.'

I agreed, indifferently. 'You seem tired,' I said.

'Department stores always give me such a headache,' she said. 'I'm going to take some aspirin.' She asked for a glass of water and some tea.

'You should see a doctor. You get too many headaches.'

'Oh I'm used to them, they come and go,' she said, diluting two pills in a glass of water. She drank it, and smiled. 'Pascal told me about your conversation,' she said. 'He was slightly hurt, because he felt that you judged him too harshly. You mustn't,' she said, looking at me gravely.

'I am not judging him harshly,' I said. I had no choice. If Andrée had to go, it was better for her to leave trusting Pascal.

'I know that I have a tendency to exaggerate,' she said; 'I think that I won't be strong enough, but we're always strong enough.' She crossed and uncrossed her fingers nervously, but her face was calm. 'All my unhappiness comes from a lack of faith. I have to believe in Maman, in Pascal, in God. Once I do, I'll know that they don't hate one another, and that they only want what's best for me.'

She seemed to be speaking more to herself than to me. It wasn't like her.

'Yes,' I said. 'You know that Pascal loves you, and that eventually you'll be married. So two years isn't very long ...'

'It's better for me to go. They're right. I know very well that the flesh is sinful; so the flesh must be fled. Let's have the courage to face up to these things,' she added.

I didn't reply. And then I did. 'Will they leave you alone, up there? Will you have some time to yourself?'

'I'll take some classes, and I'll have lots of free time.' She sipped her tea. Her hands relaxed. 'In that sense, it's an opportunity, this trip to England. In Paris I'd have led a terrible life. In Cambridge, I'll be able to catch my breath.'

'Don't forget to eat, and get some sleep,' I said.

'Don't be afraid. I'll be reasonable. But I want to apply myself,' said Andrée, in an animated voice. 'I'll read the English poets, some of them are so beautiful. Maybe I'll try to translate something. And I'd so love to write a study of the English novel. There are such interesting things to say about novels, things that no one else has said yet.' She smiled. 'My mind's a bit scrambled, I'm just having so many different ideas lately.'

'I'd love to hear about them.'

'I want to discuss them with you.' Andrée drained her cup of tea. 'Next time I'll arrange it so I have more time. I'm so sorry to have bothered you for a five-minute meeting, but I wanted to tell you not to worry about me anymore. I understand that things are just as they ought to be.'

I walked her out of the tea room and left her in front of the sweets counter. She gave me a big, encouraging smile. 'I'll ring you. See you soon!'

★★★

Pascal told me what happened next. I made him describe the scene so many times that it's difficult for me now to distinguish between what I remember and what I personally witnessed. It was two days later, towards the end of the day. Monsieur Blondel was grading at his desk; Emma was peeling vegetables; Pascal wasn't home yet. Someone rang at the door. Emma wiped her hands and went to answer it. On the other side she found a young dark-haired woman, well-dressed in a grey suit, but wearing no hat, which was, in those days, simply not done.

'I would like to speak to Monsieur Blondel,' said Andrée. Emma thought she was one of her father's former students, and brought her into his office. Monsieur Blondel was taken aback by this young woman whom he did not know, walking towards him with outstretched hand.

'Good evening, Monsieur. I'm Andrée Gallard.'

'I'm so sorry,' he said, shaking her hand, 'but I can't recall where I know you from ...?'

She sat down, and nonchalantly crossed her legs. 'Pascal hasn't mentioned me?'

'Ah! You're a friend of Pascal's?' said Monsieur Blondel.

'Not a friend.' She looked around. 'He isn't here?'

'No.'

'Where is he?' she asked, sounding worried. 'Is he already in heaven?'

Monsieur Blondel examined her more closely. Her cheeks were flushed; she clearly had a fever. 'He should be home any moment,' he said.

'It doesn't matter. You're the one I came to see,' said Andrée. She shivered. 'You're looking to see if I bear the mark of sin on my face? I promise you I'm no sinner; I have always fought against it, always,' she said, passionately.

'You seem like a very nice young lady,' Monsieur Blondel stammered, growing impatient. He was a bit deaf, into the bargain.

'I'm no saint,' she said, putting her hand to her fore-head. 'I'm no saint, but I won't hurt Pascal. I beg of you: please don't make me go!'

'Go? Go where?'

'You have no idea. Maman will send me to England if you force me to go.'

'I'm not forcing you to go anywhere,' said Monsieur Blondel. 'There's been some misunderstanding.' The word reassured him. He repeated it. 'It's a misunderstanding.'

'I know how to keep house,' said Andrée. 'Pascal won't want for anything. And I'm not some socialite. As long as I can play my violin and see Sylvie, I don't ask for anything more.' She peered at Monsieur Blondel anxiously. 'You don't think I'm unreasonable?'

'You seem eminently reasonable.'

'Then why are you against me?'

'My dear, all I can say is that there's been some misunderstanding; I am not against you,' said Monsieur Blondel. He didn't comprehend any of what was happening, but he felt pity for this fevered young woman. He wanted to reassure her, and he spoke so convincingly that Andrée's face relaxed.

'Really?'

'I swear it.'

'So you won't prevent us from having children?'

'Of course not.'

'Seven is too many,' said André, 'inevitably one of them will be a bit rubbish, but three or four is good.'

'Why don't you tell me your story,' said Monsieur Blondel.

'Yes,' said Andrée. She thought for a moment. 'You see, I told myself that I ought to have the strength to go, I told myself that I would. But this morning, when I woke up, I saw that I couldn't. So I came to ask you to take pity on me.'

'I am not your enemy,' said Monsieur Blondel. 'Tell me.'

She told him, more or less coherently. Pascal heard her voice through the door, and had quite a shock. 'Andrée!' he chastised her, coming into the room. But his father waved him off. 'Mademoiselle Gallard wanted to speak with me, and I am very glad to make her acquaintance. But she is very tired, and she has a fever; you should bring her home to her mother.'

Pascal took Andrée's hand. 'Yes, you have a fever,' he said.

'It's nothing, I'm so happy! Your father doesn't hate me!'

Pascal touched her hair. 'Wait for me. I'm going to call you a taxi.'

His father followed him into the next room, and told him what Andrée had said. 'Why didn't you tell me?' he asked, unhappily.

'I was wrong not to,' said Pascal. He began to feel something unknown, something inclement and unbearable, rising in his throat. Andrée had closed her eyes; they waited for the car in silence. He took her arm to help her down the stairs.

In the taxi she put her head on his shoulder. 'Pascal, why have you never kissed me?'

He kissed her.

Sitting by Andrée's bedside, Pascal briefly talked things over with Madame Gallard. 'You don't have to leave, it's all arranged,' said Madame Gallard.

Andrée smiled. 'Someone should order champagne,' she said. And then she sank into delirium. The doctor prescribed sedatives; he spoke of meningitis, of encephalitis, but couldn't say for sure.

I learned via pneumatic message[17] from Madame Gallard that Andrée had been delirious all night. The doctors said she should be isolated, and she was taken to a clinic in Saint-Germain-en-Laye where they tried everything they could to bring her fever down. She spent three days alone with a nurse.

'I want Pascal, Sylvie, my violin and some champagne,' she said from time to time as she rambled. The fever didn't break.

Madame Gallard watched over her the fourth night, and in the morning Andrée recognised her.

'Am I going to die?' she asked. 'I can't die before the wedding. The twins will be so adorable in that blue silk!' She was so weak she could barely speak. Several times she said 'I'm going to ruin the party! I ruin everything! All I give you is trouble.'

Later she squeezed her mother's hands. 'Don't be sad,' she said. 'In every family there's a bit of rubbish. I was the rubbish.'

---

[17] A system of sending messages by a vacuum mechanism through a system of pipes, installed in the Paris sewerage network, from one telegraph office to another. The practice was in operation until 1984.

She may have said other things, but Madame Gallard didn't repeat them to Pascal. When I rang the clinic around ten in the morning, they told me it was over. The doctors still couldn't say why.

I went to see Andrée in the chapel of the clinic. She was surrounded by candles and flowers, and wore one of her stiff cotton nightshirts. Her hair had grown out, and fell in straight locks around her yellowed face, which was so thin I had a difficult time recognising her features. Her hands, with their long pale talons, held a crucifix, and looked as fragile as those of an ancient mummy.

We buried her in the little cemetery at Béthary, alongside the dust of her ancestors. Madame Gallard sobbed. 'We have been but instruments in the hands of God,' Monsieur Gallard told her. The grave was covered in white flowers.

A dark insight occurred to me: Andrée had suffocated in all this whiteness. Atop that immaculate abundance, I lay down three red roses, before leaving for my train.

Afterword

Simone de Beauvoir was nine years old and a student at Adeline Désir, a private, Catholic institution in Paris, when a girl with short brown hair sat down beside her. Two weeks older than Simone, Elisabeth Lacoin, known as Zaza, was spontaneous, amusing and forthright – a sharp contrast to the conservative atmosphere in which they found themselves.

The next autumn, when the school year began, Zaza didn't turn up with the other girls. Darkness fell on the world; all was gloomy and oppressive, until the day when Zaza suddenly appeared, late in the term, bringing with her sunshine, joy and happiness. Simone fell under the spell of Zaza's lively intellect and many talents; she was completely enthralled by her. They competed to be top of the class, and became inseparable. Simone wasn't unhappy at home, with her beloved mother, her father whom she looked up to, and her little sister, who revered her in turn. But ten-year-old Simone was in the throes of her first great love affair: she worshipped Zaza, and shuddered at the thought of displeasing her. Of course, with the poignant vulnerability of youth, she didn't realise that it is precisely this precocious revelation that makes her situation, for us as readers, so moving, when she eventually tells their story. Her long, intimate conversations with Zaza meant the world to her. They were so corseted by their formal education that they were prevented from being overly familiar with each other (they called each other *vous*!), but in spite of this reserve, they talked like Simone had never talked to anyone. What is this feeling, conventionally labelled 'friendship', which set her tender heart ablaze with amazement and ecstasy, if not love? She understood very quickly that Zaza did not have similar feelings, and did not suspect the intensity of her own, but she was so dazzled that it did not matter.

Zaza died abruptly on the 25th of November 1929, a month before her 22nd birthday. Beauvoir would remain haunted by this sudden catastrophe for the rest of her life. For a long time, her friend would come to her in her dreams, staring at her reproachfully, her face yellowed under a pink hat. There was only one way to prevent her from slipping into oblivion: the magic of literature. Beauvoir tried four times to resuscitate Zaza: in the unpublished novels she wrote in her youth, in her story collection

When Things of the Spirit Come First, and in a deleted passage from *The Mandarins* (for which she was awarded the Prix Goncourt in 1954). That same year, she told the story again in a short novel, which she left untitled, and which has not been published until now. She was still unsatisfied by this final fictional transposition, but it would prove an essential detour to a decisive conversion from one genre to another: in 1958, she integrated the life and death of Zaza into her autobiography, her *Memoirs of a Dutiful Daughter.*

The finished novella, which Beauvoir kept in spite of the critical view she took of it, is immensely valuable. The confrontation with the absolute mystery of Zaza's death thwarts interrogation: other lines of attack must be attempted, the frame shifted, things must be put in another light. And the two different narratives look at different aspects of the mystery of Zaza. The novella focuses on the theme of deep friendship, as enigmatic as love, the kind that made Montaigne write of his relationship with La Boétie, 'Because he was he, and I was I.' Zaza became Andrée, and Simone her friend Sylvie, who tells the story in the first person. The 'inseparables' are reunited, in the narrative as in life, to face down the novel's events together; but it is Sylvie who reports them through the prism of her friendship with Andrée, which, through the play of contrasts, reveals its unresolvable ambiguities.

The choice of fiction required numerous transpositions and modifications, which need deciphering. The names of people and places as well as family compositions are not as they were in reality. Andrée Gallard stands in for Elisabeth Lacoin, and Sylvie Lepage for Simone de Beauvoir. The Gallard family (called Mabille in *Memoirs of a Dutiful Daughter*) has seven children, whereas the Lacoins had nine, six daughters and three sons. Simone de Beauvoir had only one sister, while Sylvie has two. The cours Adeline Désir is easily recognised, located in the rue Jacob, Saint-Germain-des-Prés; this is where the two girls are first baptised 'the inseparables'. Because this nickname builds a bridge between reality and fiction, it makes an appropriate name for the novella. Pascal Blondel is Maurice Merleau-Ponty (Pradelle in the *Memoirs*); in real life it was Merleau-Ponty's father who died, leaving him alone with his sister, who bore no resemblance to Emma. Meyrignac, in Limousin, becomes Sadernac, while Béthary refers to Gagnepan, one of the Lacoins' homes in the Landes (along with Haubardin), where Simone de Beauvoir stayed twice. Zaza is buried there, at Saint-Pandelon.

What was Zaza's cause of death?

Viral encephalitis, as cold scientific objectivity put it. But perhaps some fatal chain of events can be established that goes further back, tightening their hold on her existence, finally releasing her, weakened, depleted, desperate, to madness and death. As Simone de Beauvoir would have said: Zaza died of being exceptional. She was murdered; her death was a 'spiritualist crime'.

Zaza died because she tried to be herself, and because those around her believed that this was inherently bad. In the militant bourgeois Catholic milieu into which she was born on the 25th of December 1907, in her rigidly traditional family, a daughter's duty was to forget herself, to renounce personality, to adapt. Because Zaza was exceptional, she could not 'adapt' – a sinister term, which implied forcing oneself into a prefabricated system in which everyone is allocated their own cell, which is but one among many. Whatever overspills the mould will be tamped back down, or thrown away as waste. Zaza couldn't fit herself to the mould, and her singularity was crushed. Therein lies the crime. Simone de Beauvoir remembered with a kind of horror the day a family photograph was taken at Gagnepan. The children were lined up according to age, the six girls in matching blue taffeta dresses and straw hats decorated with cornflowers. Such was the role Zaza had long been expected to play: one of the youngest

Lacoin daughters. The young Simone vehemently refused this image. No, Zaza wasn't like the others, she was 'unique'. But her unexpected budding demand for freedom went against her family's deepest-held values. These they relentlessly imposed on Zaza, hunting her down with their 'social duties'. As Beauvoir depicts in the novel, surrounded by a household full of brothers and sisters, cousins, family friends, and a vast network of kin, worn down by chores, society events, visits, or collective amusements, Andrée didn't have a second to herself. She was never left alone, or alone with a friend. She did not belong to herself. She had no private time to play her violin, or to study; the privilege of solitude was denied her. This is why she found the summers in Béthary hellish. She was stifled. She wanted so badly to escape from the omnipresent crowd of people that she went so far as to hack at her foot with an axe to escape a particularly odious obligation – an act which, in a sense, resembles the mortifications practised in some religious orders. In this environment one is not allowed to be singular, or to exist for oneself; one may only exist for others. Under the relentless impregnation of these alienating traditions, any individualisation is nipped in the bud. There was nothing worse or more scandalous for Simone de Beauvoir, and that is what she wanted to explore in her novella, which we might think of as a philosophical scandal, because it is an attack on human rights themselves.

Affirming the absolute value of subjectivity would remain at the centre of her thought and her work. Not of the individual, just one of many others on a larger scale, but of unique individuality, which makes each of us 'the most irreplaceable of beings' as Gide put it, the existence of that awareness, here and now. 'Love that which you will never see twice.' An unshakeable, original conviction, which philosophical reflection bears out: the absolute is played out here on earth, during our one and only existence. Understood in this light, the stakes for Zaza could not be higher.

This tragedy was the result of several converging forces. Zaza's devotion to her mother, and her mother's unwillingness to support her, tore her apart. She loved her with a passionate, jealous, unhappy ardour, but her affection was met with a kind of coldness; Zaza, the second daughter, felt lost in the mass of siblings, one among many. Madame Lacoin shrewdly did not waste her parental authority trying to control her children's roughhousing, keeping it in reserve so that she might even more forcefully assert her control over them when it came to more important matters. In that milieu a daughter could take one of two paths, marriage or the convent; she could not choose her destiny according to her tastes and desires. It was her family who would find her a husband, by organising 'interviews', selecting candidates according to their ideo-logical, religious, social and financial objectives. One didn't marry outside of one's caste. When she was fifteen, Zaza had her first encounter with this deadly dogma: she was brutally separated from her cousin with whom she had fallen in love; and at twenty the same thing threatened to happen again. Hoping to marry an outsider such as Pascal Blondel was a misdemeanour, and as such, unacceptable in her family's eyes. Zaza's tragedy was that deep down, she was self-defeating: she didn't have the courage to stand up to a sacred, beloved authority, whose reproachfulness was killing her. At the very moment when her mother's disapproval was eating away at her self-confidence and her zest for life, she went almost as far as to submit to the wisdom of the judge who condemned her. Madame Lacoin's repression of her daughter was even more para-doxical given that when she herself was a girl, she had been, it seems, forced to marry someone she detested. She had to 'adapt' – that's when the atrocious word first appeared – and renounce her earlier feelings; then, on becoming a matriarch herself, she elected to perpetuate a cycle from which she herself had found no escape. What frustration and resentment did she hide behind her self-composure?

Piety, or rather a social doctrine of spiritualism, weighed on Zaza's ambitions. Religion saturated her life: she was the daughter of militant Catholics, her father was the president of the League of Fathers of Large Families; her mother played a prominent role in the parish of Saint-Thomas-d'Aquin; one of her brothers was a priest, and one of her sisters a nun. Every year the family made a pilgrimage to Lourdes. What Simone de Beauvoir denounces as 'spiritualism' is the 'blancheur', or whiteness, of religion, the process by which it casts a heavenly veil over extremely earthly values and concerns. Of course, those who mystify are the first to be mystified. Religion is reflexively employed to justify anything and everything. 'We have been but instruments in the hands of God,' says Monsieur Gallard after his daughter's death. Zaza was made to submit because she had internalised a Catholicism which most people practise at their convenience, as a formality. Being exceptional, yet again, worked against her. Although she was well aware of the hypocrisy, the lies and the egotistical 'moralism' of those in her milieu, whose petty, purely self-serving thoughts and actions constantly betrayed the spirit of the Gospels, her faith, though shaken, persisted. But she suffered from internal exile, the inability to understand those closest to her, and from the loneliness – although she was never alone – of existential solitude. The sincerity of her spiritual standards mortified her, in the fullest sense of the word, and tortured her; she found herself cornered by her own personal contradictions.

Because for Zaza, faith was not, as it is for many, a smug exploitation of God, a way of being right, of self-justifying and fleeing one's responsibilities, but the painful questioning of a God who remained silent, obscure, hidden. She was her own executioner, and it tore her apart: should she obey, submit, stop thinking about herself, stop questioning everything, the way her mother insisted she must? Or should she disobey, revolt, lay claim to the talents and gifts that had been bestowed upon her, as her best friend encouraged her to do? What was God's will? What did He expect of her?

Her fear of sinning sapped her vitality. Unlike Sylvie, Andrée/Zaza is well aware of the temptations of the body. Madame Gallard, with an almost sadistic brutality, informed her fifteen-year-old daughter of the cruder aspects of marriage. The wedding night, she told her, in no uncertain terms, was an uncomfortable moment to be endured. Zaza's own experience belied this cynicism; she had experienced the magic of sexuality, and desire; the kisses Andrée exchanges with Bernard are not platonic. She mocks the sentimental idiocy of the virginal young women that surround her, the hypocrisy of those who self-righteously 'whitewash', deny, or conceal the crude needs of the body. But inversely, she knows she is vulnerable to temptation, and her blazing sensuality, ardent temperament and voluptuous love of life are poisoned by her excessive scruples. In the slightest hint of desire she suspects a sin: the sin of the flesh. Remorse, fear and guilt cripple her, and this self-condemnation reinforces the allure of giving up, the fascination with the void, and other worryingly self-destructive tendencies. Andrée finally gives in to her mother's wishes, and those of Pascal, who persuades her that a too-long engagement would be dangerous, and agrees to exile in England even though her entire being is in revolt against the idea. This final, savage constraint – employed against herself – brings on the ultimate catastrophe. Andrée dies, drawn and quartered by all of these contradictions.

In the novella, Sylvie's role as Andrée's friend is simply to make us understand her. As Éliane Lecarme-Tabone rightly points out, few of her own memories appear, we learn little of her own life and struggles, the eventful story of her liberation, or, especially, of the fundamental antagonism that existed between intellectuals and self-righteous believers – the central theme of *Memoirs of a Dutiful Daughter*. These issues are loosely sketched out here. Still, it becomes clear that she is looked down upon in Andrée's social circle, and barely tolerated. While the Gallards enjoy comfortable financial circumstances, Sylvie's own family, which at the opening of the novel rests squarely within the bourgeoisie, loses all their money and status in the First World War. Sylvie is politely humiliated when she visits Andrée's family at Béthary: she is made aware that her hair and her clothing are not quite *comme il faut*; Andrée discreetly hangs a pretty dress in her wardrobe. But worse, Madame Gallard herself is wary of Sylvie, this wayward young woman who studies at the Sorbonne, who will have a career, earn money and be independent. The heart-rending scene in the kitchen, where Sylvie reveals to a flabbergasted Andrée what she has meant to her – everything – is a turning point in their friendship, when their roles reverse. From then on, it will be Andrée who cares more. The world and all it has to offer is opening up before Sylvie, while Andrée is heading towards death. But Sylvie/Simone will bring Andrée back to life, with tenderness and respect, through the grace of literature. I can't help pointing out that [in French] the four parts of *Memoirs of a Dutiful Daughter* end on the following words: 'Zaza', '*raconterais* [would tell]', '*mort* [death]', and '*sa mort* [her death]'.[18] Simone de Beauvoir would feel guilty, because in a way, surviving was a crime. Zaza was the price she paid, as she says in some of her unpublished notes, 'the hostage' taken in exchange for her escape. But for us, the novella fulfils the almost sacred task that she

---

[18] In English they end on 'Zaza', 'a story I would make up as I went along', 'death' and 'her death'.

attributed to literature: to fight against time, against forgetting, against death, to 'do justice to this absolute presence of the instant, to this eternity of the instant, which will have been forever'.

Sylvie Le Bon de Beauvoir, 2020

Translated by Lauren Elkin, 2021
Revised by Vintage Classics, 2021

Archive Material

The Lacoin family circa 1923 at Haubardin. Zaza is in the second row, 4th from the left.

Simone in 1915, shortly before she met Zaza.

Portrait of Zaza, 1928.

Maurice Merleau-Ponty, Zaza's great love, called Pascal in the novel.

Left to right: Zaza, Simone, and Geneviève de Neuville, at Gagnepan, September 1928. Zaza and Simone had been friends since the age of ten, when they met at the Cours Désir in Paris.

Zaza and Simone at Gagnepan, September 1928.

The first and fourth pages of a letter Simone wrote to Zaza when they were twelve years old, written in violet ink, signed "Your inseparable."

"My dear Zaza, I firmly believe that my lassitude is equalled only by your own; I received your wonderful letter fifteen days ago and still haven't put my mind to replying until now. I am having such fun here that I simply haven't found the time. I've just come back from the hunt; it was my third time going out. But I've had no luck: my uncle hasn't killed anything the days I've gone with him. Today he hit a partridge but it fell into a bush and not having [...]"

"not at all. Are there blackberries at Gagnepan? At Meyrignac we have loads, they cover the hedges, and we gorge ourselves on them. Goodbye my dear Zaza, don't make me wait as long for your letter as you've had to wait for mine. I embrace you with all my heart, as well as your brothers and sisters and especially your godson. Please pay my respects to Madame Lecoin; Maman sends hers as well. Your inseparable, Simone. Decipher these scribblings if you can."

Letter from Zaza to Simone, 3rd September 1927, in which she describes wounding herself with an axe in order to get away from the bustle and stress of Gagnepan.

My dear Simone,

Your letter reached me at a time when I had some time to myself to reflect, which brought me much of the lucidity and understanding that I could not find during the first part of our stay here. I felt such joy reading you, feeling that we were very close to one another, whereas your previous letter had made me feel that you were growing distant from me, and suddenly forging a different path. In short, please forgive me for having very badly misunderstood. My mistake arose from the fact that in your previous letter you emphasized your pursuit of truth, your most recent conquest; that is to say, I thought I saw in this achievement, which is only one goal, only one way of giving meaning to your life, a renunciation of everything else, and an abandonment of such a beautiful part of our humanity. I see that this kind of mutilation is not at all what you had in mind, and that you have renounced none of yourself; that, I am now convinced, is where the true energy lies, and I believe it is necessary to force ourselves to reach a certain point of internal perfection where all our contradictions melt away, and where we may become ourselves in all our vastness. And that is why I particularly liked the way you said "save oneself whole and intact" which is the most beautiful human conception of existence, and which isn't so very far off from the Christian idea of "seeking salvation" when you understand it in its larger meaning.

Although you didn't say so, I know that a great feeling of peace has settled within you, merely from the way your letter calmed me. There is no feeling in the world more sweet than knowing that there is someone who understands you entirely, and upon whose friendship one may count absolutely.

Come as quickly as you can; the 10th, for instance, is convenient for us, as is any other date for that matter. You will be here at the same time as the de Neuvilles, who will be here from the 8th to the 15th; no doubt your first days here will be very busy, but I believe that you will stay on much longer after they've gone, and that you will enjoy Gagnepan in its calm moments as well as its agitated ones. I suspect when I said "amuse oneself in order to forget it all," you sought to reproach me, and I would like to explain myself, as I have gone well beyond my thoughts. I know from experience that there are moments when nothing can distract me from my thoughts and that trying to amuse myself is an ordeal. Recently, at Haubardin, they organized a great excursion with some friends to the Netherlands; I felt such a keen need for solitude at that moment that amusing myself would have been impossible, and I hacked myself in the foot with an axe so as to have an excuse not to go. That won me eight days of bedrest and loads of pity from everyone, as well as a few comments about my carelessness and clumsiness, but at least I had a bit of time alone, and the right to not speak to anyone or have to amuse myself.

I very much hope I won't have to resort to the axe again during your visit; on the 11th we've decided to journey about twenty-five kilometers from here to see a cattle race and we'll also stop in at an old château where some cousins of ours are staying. Do try to be here for it, I beg you. As for your train, I don't know what to tell you. Come via Bordeaux or Montauban? If it's Montaubon, we can pick you up at Riscle, which isn't far from here, to spare you changing trains. Take whichever one you want, I'll come at any time of day or night to pick you up in our motorcar. But do come quickly.

Farewell my dear Simone, I am yours with all my heart. [Illegible word: Send? or Pass on?] my respects to your mother and tell her how grateful I am for allowing you to come here.

Zaza

First page of the manuscript of The Inseparables, *written in* 1954.